Jump and Dance

JUMP AND DANCE

JOHN WALKER

Matador
9 Priory Business Park,
Wistow Road, Kibworth Beauchamp,
Leicestershire, LE8 0RX
Tel: 0116 279 2299
Email: books@troubador.co.uk
Web: www.troubador.co.uk/matador
Twitter: @matadorbooks

ISBN 978 1789013 115

British Library Cataloguing in Publication Data.
A catalogue record for this book is available from the British Library.

Printed and bound in the UK by 4edge limited
Typeset in 11pt Minion Pro by Troubador Publishing Ltd, Leicester, UK

Matador is an imprint of Troubador Publishing Ltd

For Laura
I cherish the memories until we meet again
True love never dies
To the wonderful music of the 1960's
Thank you

A percentage from the sale of this book will go to Cancer Research.

Chapter One

Some bird once told me I was narcissism personified. I hadn't the faintest idea what she meant, if it was good or bad, a compliment or a criticism. When I got home I looked it up in my old school dictionary – Narcissism: abnormal self-love or self-admiration. *Fuck, what was wrong with that,* I told my reflection in the mirror.

It had definitely been the best day of my life so far. That very morning sitting on the top deck of the number ninety on my way to work, only the number one Mod, the fucking top man himself, Seg, had turned around and offered me a cigarette. Even though I had just quit smoking, I still took one. A couple of times before he'd nodded his head at me in acknowledgement, one Mod to another. But this – how cool could you get? Seg wore a full length red leather coat to work; I mean fucking hell. Here I was sharing a smoke with him; he handed me his cigarette and I lit mine off the glowing end. Thanks, man. I handed him back his cigarette, trying to be so nonchalant. He winked at me and turned around. I studied the back of his head, his blonde, almost white, carefully styled hair.

Shit, he had hair to die for. Fucking hell, just wait until I told Roothy. He was already green with envy knowing that every day I rode the same bus as him.

It was the summer of nineteen sixty-six, and it seemed just about anything was possible: the style, the girls, the music, football, England World Cup winners. There were kids playing football on every patch of grass and after dark on the street under the lampposts. World Cup Willie was the cry of the nation, and you just knew Lonnie Donegan hated himself. I should have been on top of the world like everyone else seemed to be, but the trouble was I had this crappy job that I hated – Apprentice Bender – it sounded like a job for a queer. Seven months I'd been there, since leaving school at Christmas, and now here I was again sitting on the bus going to this boring job I hated. I still didn't know what the pipes were for, and I wasn't really interested. The only thing I knew for certain was that they were fucking big pipes. Just the week before I had started working there, some bloke had been crushed by one of these pipes. Squashed like a gnat right in the shop where I worked. They say they had to roll him up like a carpet when the ambulance came to take him away, he was that flat. They had these two overhead cranes that moved the pipes, one driven by some Polish bloke, the other by a West Indian. Both of them as thick as two short planks, both fucking head cases, especially the Polack. It was the Pole who dropped the pipe on the bloke. Still, it looked a great job, climbing up to that little cab and flying around the roof all day.

Mick and Teddy were already there, sitting on a workbench smoking. Arthur, who was in charge of our little section, had already started work; the clock on the wall said five to seven. Company man, I said, nodding in the direction of Arthur and joining the other two on the bench. Fucking twat, was Mick's opinion. That man would work for nothing. Mick was a year older than me and Teddy: a Greabo; well, not really a Greabo, more the original Hippie. He had really long hair, and I envied the fact nothing seemed to bother him. Mick was a good mate and a good bloke. I'll tell you something, Teddy laughed, stubbing out his cigarette and putting it behind his ear. If you saw his missus you'd be begging them to let you work seven days a week, even for fucking nothing. Teddy was going out with this girl Mary, who worked in the offices; they were real serious. Actually, Mary was quite fit, but they were already talking about getting engaged. They were so young and always seemed so serious. Why the rush? I just couldn't understand them. The seven o'clock siren deafened the conversation, sounding like an air raid warning. Arthur, who had been in the Home Guard during the war, took a quick glance up at the roof. He could have been checking for the Luftwaffe or falling pipes. Never mind, lads, only five hours till footy Mick, shouted over the din of a hundred hammers falling on metal.

Thinking about it, the only good thing about the job was the game of football we had every dinnertime. It was always Blacks versus Whites – not shirt colour, skin colour. A few of the Polacks were always hanging around trying to get a game with our side. Stan, who was our self-appointed captain, and an ex pro according to him, told them to piss off. We're white, they protested. That don't matter, Stan told, them you're fucking foreign, ain't yer? Nobody argued with Stan; he was a right hard bastard. The Polacks tried the Blacks, but they didn't want them either.

I was saving up to buy a scooter, a Lambretta 150cc, but trying to save money on an apprentice's wages was just about impossible. My sister's boyfriend had a Lambretta, although he wasn't a Mod. In fact he was a right tosser, trapped in a Teddy boy time warp. But sometimes when he came around I have to admit that he looked pretty cool, from his duck's arse hair to his beetle crushers. If I had been ten years older I would definitely have been a Ted. Maybe just for the luminous pink and yellow socks and the velvet collars. Just a week before my sixteenth birthday, I persuaded him to let me have a go on his scooter. It was a quiet Sunday afternoon on a deserted country lane; the slight kick back as the gears engaged let me know only the brake was holding me. The machine under me had come alive; I let the brake out gently and at the same time twisted the throttle back. Gliding smoothly away lifting my feet off the tarmac like a kid riding a bike for the very first time. Fuck, I hadn't even gone twenty yards when this cop car came out of fucking nowhere and pulled alongside me. Kinross was grinning at me through the window, motioning for me to stop. This, I knew, was payback time. He got out of his car and put his peaked cap on his head; he looked like the fucking Gestapo, and I thought about giving him a Heil Hitler. Licence, he smirked, taking out his notebook and licking his pencil.

Kinross lived opposite our house; there was a big board in the front garden advertising the fact that a copper lived there. It was known locally as the Pig Sty. There was a recreation ground separating two rows of houses; the posh semis on one side called it the Village Green; to the doorsteppers on the other side it was the Rec. Football was religiously played on the Rec in the winter and cricket in the summer. The kids still played there, but now we were older the only time we used the Rec was after dark, gathering around the swings in the far corner, smoking, and copping a feel of some girl's tits if we were lucky.

Two summers earlier, just before Girls became more important than football or cricket, the sun had turned the grass wiry brown and the wicket a baked mud strip with cracks wide enough to stick your fingers in. Everybody was a fast bowler, and a cricket ball bouncing up off that rock-hard strip could do serious damage. I was batting, and my cousin, who was better at football and cricket than any of us, was on his huge run-up and about to unleash the ball. Closing my eyes I took a huge swing, and instead of finding the stumps shattered I connected with the middle of the bat. Opening my eyes I watched the ball clear the wall for six and straight into the door of Kinross's shiny new patrol car as he was driving past. Just for a moment time stood still, the dull thud of the cricket ball hitting the metal drifted across the warm summer breeze, and everyone seemed mesmerised as the ball slowly ran down the road. A loud shout of Fucking Run brought the world back to real time and everyone scattered, but he knew it was me. You didn't make sergeant for nothing. That evening he pulled up outside our house with a lovely big dent in the door. We all went out to inspect it, and Dad was most apologetic, much to my dismay. Kinross ranted and raved, and threatened this and that, but there was nothing he could do. Are you finished? Dad asked him. Well, get in your car and piss off, and be more careful in future. Come on, lad, don't worry, you've done nothing wrong. We went back inside, leaving Kinross looking as though at any minute he might explode.

Kinross had waited patiently for two years, and now he had me bang to rights. By the time the case went to court almost three months later, a lot of things had changed. I now had a scooter of my own, not the Lambretta that I had set my heart on, but a Vespa 125cc. It was a case of beggars can't be choosers. Dad had lent me the money to buy it, otherwise I would have been the only serious Mod in town without one. It had a chrome front rack, chrome backrest, and four mirrors; I told myself that Lambrettas were bad luck.

Kinross was sitting on a wooden bench in the corridor outside the courtroom; we sat down opposite. Morning, the smug bastard said, grinning from ear to ear. He was all decked out in his best uniform as though he had an appointment with the Queen to be knighted. His silver buttons gleamed brightly in the autumn sunshine pouring through the window; I was sure he had been up all night polishing them. When the clerk called out our names, he took his cap from the bench and gave the peak one final polish with his elbow. Jesus Christ, I couldn't believe it. The gallery on either side was packed with all the kids from school, all my old classmates. What the fuck was going on? What were they doing here? Had word somehow got around that I was up before the judge? Maybe they had organised a trip just to come and have a laugh. All heads turned as I walked between them. I could see a couple of the girls, their hands up to their mouths stifling a giggle. Old Oscar was sitting on the end of the aisle. Be quiet, he hissed at the class as I walked by. He turned around and our eyes met: the look he gave me was pure disgust. I could almost hear him thinking, *I knew he was a wrong un.* He never did like me, the little Welsh twat; still, I wished I was sitting in one of his boring classes right now instead of being here.

Kinross had his moment first, and swore to tell the whole truth and nothing but the truth, and then proceeded to tell a pack of lies. He said that he had followed me for half a mile, and that I had been driving erratically. The judge asked me if I had anything to say, although it obviously pained him to actually speak to me. He squinted at me over his half-moon glasses as though I was the lowest of the low – a rapist, even a murderer perhaps. My sister's boyfriend had warned me not to say anything apart from yes and no. He said the judge was a right bastard, which made me wonder just who exactly she was going out with. It looked to me as though he'd been here before. It must have been the way he looked at me, because I couldn't stop myself. Most of what he just told you were lies, I said pointing at Kinross. For a start, it was nearer half a yard than half a mile. The judge, who must have been eighty if he was a day, jumped to his feet like someone much younger. Silence. Silence! he shouted. I will not stand for this insolent behaviour in my courtroom. Take your hands out of your pockets and stand up straight. Instinctively I did as he said, while wondering at the same time just what my posture had to do with any of this. Young man, I don't think you realise the seriousness of this offence. It is quite within the jurisdiction of this court to send you to a young offender institution. Any more outbursts like that, and I would be forced to consider it. Although it seems to me a spell in the armed services might be better, he mumbled. That really struck a nerve; my old man had been on the *King George the V* when she sank the *Bismarck*. This old fart had probably been sat behind a desk, safe and sound. I was just about to ask him, when I felt a sharp jab in the ribs from my sister's boyfriend who was standing next to me; I got the message and kept quiet. We were both fined twelve pounds and had our licences endorsed.

Since I had got the scooter, I was no longer using the bus to work. The job wasn't really going too well; the money just wasn't enough for the things I wanted. Friday was okay though – that was day release at college, and it was just like being back at school, messing about all day. The trouble was, I should have been going to night classes every Tuesday, but I'd only been once, and that was only to enrol. Anyway, I had better things to do. Sooner or later someone was going to notice and inform the company: now that time had come. I had heard a rumour that I was to be called into the office, but I was already one step ahead. I had got myself another job. When they sent for me, I handed them my notice. The job was at the foundry where my dad worked. I hadn't even told him. Shit, he would go mad and try to talk me out of it, tell me I was throwing my life away. But that was just it: it was my life, and the money was more than three times what I was earning now.

On the Friday, my last day as an apprentice pipe bender, I stayed at home. The thought of all those awkward goodbyes, especially to Mick and Teddy, was something I didn't need. Saturday night, I saw Teddy and Mary in town. They told me Mick was dead. Thursday night on his way home from work, he had lost control of his motorbike on a bend, clipping the kerb; he was thrown across the road and under the wheels of a lorry. Right there in the middle of town on a busy Saturday night, I thought about death for the first time. Grandma and Grandad had died within a few months of each other, but I was only ten years old. Somehow, back then, nothing had changed, in my life anyway. I just didn't see them anymore, and no more Sunday visits. We stood in silence while all around happy people walked by laughing and joking, and life just went on. I wanted to scream at them to stop, until I saw that Mary was crying. I looked at Teddy, but he didn't seem to notice. Slowly I put my arms around her, but the words I needed to say to comfort her would not come. Instead they lay unspoken on the tip of my tongue, as my awkwardness became lost in her very closeness. She smelt so young and fresh, new and beautiful. I wanted to hold her in my arms forever and never let her go. I wished she were my girl, I felt so much love for her. Suddenly, love and death, death and love, became the same thing. I silently let her go and punched

Teddy playfully on the arm. We said our goodbyes, and he promised to let me know when the funeral was.

The rest of the weekend I stayed at home, the thought of Mick lifeless on some stone slab constant in my mind. The thought of Mary wrapped in my arms, her very closeness still on my skin and my clothes. Sunday night I told my dad I would be going to work with him in the morning. Instead of ranting and raving, he just gave me a look. It was a look of abject disappointment, which for a while made me think I was doing the wrong thing. The funeral was on Thursday. Taking time off work so soon after starting didn't go down too well, but fuck it, the job was shit anyway. It was going to be short-term. This was the first funeral I had ever been to. They played *Stay,* not by The Hollies, but by Maurice Williams and The Zodiacs. It was fucking ace. *Oh, won't you stay just a little bit longer;* fucking hell, Mick. I sat with Teddy and Mary in the church.

Mary had on a black short skirt suit, and I could not stop looking at her legs. Somehow the whole thing was surreal, like some kind of dream. I was wearing a navy blue suit with a fourteen-inch centre vent; it was from Burtons off the peg but I told everyone I had it made to measure. Outside I swallowed a couple more of the pills Roothy had given me. I don't know what the fuck they were but I was flying.He said they were nicked from his Grandma's bathroom cabinet. Was I the top man sitting astride the Vespa with everyone looking at me? Saying goodbye to Mary and Teddy, Mary leaned in close and kissed my cheek. I knew I probably would not see them again; I know they were thinking the same. Mary's hand touched my cheek as she rubbed away her lipstick. Unspoken words passed between us, and I rode away with her beautiful sweet scent all around me. Somewhere out there was a girl like that just waiting for me, there just had to be.

Chapter Two

At last I was earning some money, just to be able to go out with my mates on equal terms and pay my own way was a great feeling. Bank Holiday Monday, we caught the train for a day in Skegness. Roothy's scooter was out of action, and Omo didn't have one, so the train it was. What a day it was; I saw Tommy in a bar on the seafront. When we were kids Tommy and me had been inseparable, until he passed his eleven plus and I failed mine. I couldn't believe it he was a fucking top Mod. Tommy gave us all a little pick-me-up, handing out bennies like fucking sweets. He said he knew this bird that worked in Boots. Fuck, we were soon flying, and when they were gone we bought some of our own from this fucking Gypo under the prom. The bastard sold us some bad shit, which Omo sold to some little pretend Mods for more than what we paid for it. It had been a great day, even though we hadn't pulled. There were no seats on the train going home: it was packed, standing room only. Three-quarters of the train were either pissed or stoned, or both. The atmosphere was electric frightening and edgy, but at the same time friendly and fun. A gorgeous looking girl with jet-black hair in a black and white pop art dress offered me her seat and said she would sit on my lap. It was an offer too good to refuse. Her name was Jenny, and she was from Nottingham. In between snogging, she told me her boyfriend had gone to London to see The Who. Not to be outdone, I told her I'd already seen them. Jenny's kisses became more passionate, her tongue lingering in my mouth. She seemed suitably impressed by this information, even though it was a downright lie. The closest I had come to seeing The Who was on *Ready Steady Go*. As the train shuddered to a halt at another station, I looked out the window to see where we were. The sign said Beeston: just a couple more stops before Nottingham. I hadn't seen Roothy or Omo since Jenny had sat on my lap. Jenny stuck her tongue down my throat as the train slowly left the station behind. My right leg had gone to sleep ages ago, and now the left one was aching like hell. There was no way I was going to move, even if I never walked again; I had my hand on Jenny's left tit.

Fucking hell Jonty, Roothy said, pulling at my arm. Fucking hell, he said again. Omo appeared beside him grinning down at me. Fuck, you missed it, Roothy laughed. Missed what, I asked, losing my grip on Jenny as she turned around on my lap. Omo just belted some nigger. What? I said, finally losing my hold on Jenny's tit. Fucking black bastard, Omo spat. What did you do? Jenny asked him. I leaned out the window as we were pulling out of the station, and just cracked the black bastard. He went down like a fucking sack of shit. Roothy added: He probably swallowed his fucking whistle. Jenny and her friends all started to laugh. Fuck, don't tell me it was the fucking guard you hit. Fucked if I know, Omo shrugged. Niggers all look the same to me, but he was wearing a uniform. By the time we pulled into Nottingham ten minutes later the whole train knew about Omo smacking the guard. He was a real hero and loving every minute of it.

The cops were on the platform waiting – fucking loads of them. They kept everyone on the train. Fuck, they're coming on, and that blackie's with them, someone shouted. The pigs posted guards on all the doors, while the rest pushed their way through the crowded carriages, the nigger in between them. Omo's grin had long since disappeared; he looked as though he was about to shit himself as they came closer. Without a word Jenny got off my lap, pulled me up and pushed Omo down on the seat. She quickly sat on his knee and draped her arms around his neck. They moved by without a second glance: what a girl.

Out on the platform Jenny wrote her phone number on a scrap of paper and pushed it into my hand. We kissed for the last time, and I watched her walk away with her friends. I looked down at the piece of paper and said the number to myself a couple of times. It was the first time anyone had given me a phone number. In fact, I didn't even know anybody who had a phone, except the bloke at the end of our street. *Jesus, she must be loaded,* I thought.

It was just after ten when we pulled up at our local station, after a half-hour wait for a connecting train. The single platform was deserted – apart from a couple snogging on a bench in front of the locked waiting room. Suddenly we had all come back down to earth, such an empty feeling, and such a downer. We trudged slowly and silently up the ramp that led out of the station, back to reality, back to work in the morning. At the top of the ramp Roothy and Omo turned right, and I headed up the steps and over the old iron bridge that spanned the track. The bridge still had its original wooden slats that were loose and cracked beneath your feet, the lines below clearly visible. When I was a kid I was scared silly of this bridge. If I had to cross it I would run like crazy; if a train passed when you were halfway across, the bridge shook so much you thought it surely had to fall down. A dirty old goods train was steaming through now, so I hung back. I told myself I didn't want my new shirt covered in smoke and soot. Roothy shouted something, and Omo was killing himself laughing. I couldn't hear what he'd said so I grinned like a maniac and gave them two fingers.

On the walk home I was thinking about Jenny, feeling in my pocket for the piece of paper she had given me. I knew that I wouldn't ring her; she already had a boyfriend, and Nottingham might as well have been a thousand miles away.

So did Mary. Lost in these thoughts I didn't hear someone shouting my name. Are you deaf? she smiled breathlessly. I've been shouting for you to wait for ages.

It was a girl called Liz who lived just around the corner from me. You don't mind if I walk up with you, she said, looping her arm through mine. It was a good job it was dark and late at night; I wouldn't want anyone seeing us together. No, course I don't, I said, looking her up and down. Liz was the same age as me, she wasn't too bad looking, but she was short and plump. It felt sort of nice walking along with a girl on my arm. I took another look at her, and she smiled up at me. She had a lovely smile, and her tits were huge. There had been rumours going around that she would let anyone fuck her, but I had heard the same rumour about lots of girls and most of them were not true. Where you been? she asked, holding my arm a little tighter. Skeggy, I told her. Honest? she said, as though it was something really cool. She seemed really impressed, and her tits looked even bigger. Liz was chatting away as we walked slowly home, but I wasn't hearing much of it. My mind was trying to think of a way to get to play with her tits. *Maybe I should just come out with it: Liz, do you mind if I have a bit of a play around with your tits?* Do you want one? I heard her say through my thoughts. She was holding a pack of cigarettes in front of me. I was about to say no when I noticed they were menthol, so I took one. We were getting very close to the end of her street, and I was starting to panic. I just couldn't think of an excuse to keep her from going in. Do you fancy going down to the Rec and sitting on the swings awhile? she said in answer to my desperation. *Fucking hell, there is a God after all,* I thought to myself. Yeah, I don't mind, I replied nonchalantly.

The grass was damp and so was her cunt. I had two fingers in her, and she was moaning with pleasure and trying to get my dick out. Fuck me, Jonty, she breathed between wet sloppy kisses, please fuck me. She put it in for me. The thought that I had no protection and I might get her pregnant or, even worse, get a dose of the pox or something, briefly crossed my mind; after all, she did have a reputation. Even if I had sat up and thought about it for ten minutes, I just wouldn't have been able to stop myself. Her silky warm wetness completely surrounded me, taking me from the edge of heaven to the edge of something else. It was a place I wanted to stay forever, knowing I could not move. Underneath me her body began to take me over the edge. And the lack of willpower I had shown just a few minutes earlier came crashing into my brain. I pushed myself off her and rolled onto my back, cumming at the same time. I lay motionless looking up into the starlit sky. She raised herself up on one elbow and looked at me. Was that nice? she said in a dreamy faraway voice. Fucking hell, yes, I smiled, turning to look at her. Even in the starlight I could see her nipples erect under her top. Shit, I'd never even felt those great looking tits. Was that the first time? she asked me. No, I lied. What about you? I said, sitting up. She shook her head no.

This is the second time tonight, she said, matter of factly. She pushed me back down and started to play with my dick, which had come alive again at the thought of those great tits. I pushed myself up again, but she didn't let go. What! Who! I mean, who with? I stammered. Vince, she said. Vince, I repeated parrot fashion; not Vince Clarke. She nodded yes. Fucking hell, Vince Clarke was a right head case; he'd spent time in Borstal. Is he your boyfriend? I asked her, already knowing the answer. Yes, Vince and me are in love, she said, still rubbing my dick. Vince was about twenty-one, he rode a 500cc Norton and carried a flick knife. At that moment I didn't know what scared me the most: a good hiding from Vince if he found out that I'd fucked his girlfriend or the fact that I had most probably caught a dose if he had fucked her just before me. Liz had given up on my dick, which had suddenly gone limp at the thought of my fate. When will I see you again? she asked me. I looked at her; was she insane? What about Vince, you know, your boyfriend? I reminded her. Well, he's not really my boyfriend, she said; I just see him every now and then. Well, that's all right then, I said sarcastically. But she didn't hear me; she was crawling about on all fours looking for her knickers. It's getting cold, she said, finding them and pulling them up. She was right, and I was still naked from the waist down. I didn't want to kiss her, but I knew she wanted me to. It was a half-hearted kiss I didn't want to build her hopes up too much. And yet she would be handy if I fancied a quick shag; if Vince could do it so could I. I told her I'd probably see her in town at the weekend. She seemed quite happy with this feeble excuse. I made a mental note to buy some Durex and ran the rest of the way home.

What have you got all over your shirt? mum said. She was in the kitchen making my dad's snap for work. I looked down at the new black tab collar shirt I was wearing. Fuck, I could have died. I had cum all over myself, right down the front of my shirt. Cuckoo spit, I said, saying the first thing that came to mind. She looked at me quizzically. Come here, let's see if I can get it off. It's okay, I said, grabbing the cloth out of her hand. I can do it.

Chapter Three

My dad had been going on about football again. It's not too late he was telling me, you've still got a chance, it's better than working for a living. He was right but I just couldn't be bothered. I had been on Derby's books during my last year at school. Every Tuesday and Thursday night I had been going training, catching two buses to get there. Eventually I had stopped going. I still went out with my football kit in my bag, but I was really going out with Roothy and Omo. Girls and drinking had become more important than football. When my dad found out, it wasn't as bad as I had expected. It's your life, you do what you want with it, he told me, but you're wasting it. Somehow I sort of felt guilty, so I joined the local non-league team just to please him. It was okay. I was even getting paid a fiver expenses every game. We were playing at home the Saturday after the Skegness trip. I was feeling a lot better: no scabs or rashes had appeared on my dick, and I had managed to avoid Liz. Roothy was in the crowd at the back of the goal where we were warming up; I went over and sat on the rail talking to him as the teams were being announced over the crackling tannoy. Over at the side of the pitch the manager was waving his arms at me and shouting something. I knew he was telling me to warm up with the rest of the team, but I pretended not to hear him. He took it all too seriously; it was only a fucking game.

Two little boys with black and gold scarves wrapped around their necks had appeared by our side. When I smiled at them they held out their autograph books. I signed them but I felt really embarrassed. Roothy was pissing himself. Have you seen who's here? he said when he'd stopped laughing. Yeah, I've already seen her, I told him. Jill Brown had been to the last three home games. God, she was drop dead gorgeous. Jill was a year younger than me; she was in her final year at school. She was with a dark-haired girl who I didn't know. I watched as they stopped by the corner and leaned on the rail, looking for all the world like regular football supporters. I really hoped she wasn't coming to watch the football; I hoped she was coming to see me. Somewhere there was a girl like that for me, I reminded myself. I told Roothy to go and ask her if she fancied going out with me tonight. Fuck off, he said, ask her yourself. Geoff Wharton, our centre half and captain, was shouting at me: we were changing ends. Come on, Roothy, you know I'd do it for you, I pleaded, getting off the rail. I sprinted down to the other end, and the ref blew his whistle. It turned out to be a great afternoon; we won three one. I scored one and laid on the other two. The manager forgave me, and at half time Roothy told me that Jill had said yes.

A scout from Notts. County was waiting for me outside the changing rooms after the match. He asked me to go along for a trial on Wednesday night. I wasn't really bothered but I told him I would be there. What did she say? I asked Roothy after he'd gone. We're seeing them at seven o'clock in the Duke, he said, looking pleased with himself. We? Who's we? I asked him. I'm seeing her friend Susan, he smiled. Apparently they came here for Susan to ask you if you would go out with Jill, and for Jill to ask me if I would go out with Susan. Fuck me, would you believe it? Now, that's fate, I laughed, enjoying the moment. Getting ready that night I washed my hair twice, and left for our date with it still soaking wet. You'll catch your death; get back and dry your hair, Mum said, following me to the door. Walking down the road on my way to meet Jill for our first date, I had the feeling that this was something different, something real and deep. Jill was all I knew she would be, and now I could understand how Teddy felt about Mary. I thought about Jill every waking minute and dreamt about her almost every night. This had to be love, so much in love it hurt, a wonderful hurt. I never turned up for the Notts. County trial football – just never stood a chance. But when everything in your life is so wonderful there are always those little nagging doubts in the back of your mind that anytime soon it could all come crashing down. Nothing this good could last forever. Just over three months after our first date something happened.

The scooter was in dock for the time being, covered over with an old sheet, looking sad and forlorn in the back yard. I had only risked taking Jill on the back a couple of times, since I'd managed to get another endorsement on my licence. This time I got caught carrying Roothy on the back after we'd been ten-pin bowling in town. We were stopped at a red light, when this copper stepped out from nowhere. Just like Kinross had. They all must be trained to creep up on unsuspecting people, the sad bastard. Pull over onto the side, lad, he said. Licence, he smirked. That was another thing – they all had the same stupid grin. He held out his hand. I don't have it on me, I told him, which was true. All right, take it to your local police station in the next twenty-four hours, unless of course there is something you want to tell me, he added with the smirk back again on his face. I just looked at him. Okay, let's put it another way – have you passed your test, because if you haven't we will find out tomorrow, won't we? I glanced at Roothy; he gave me a resigned look and shrugged his shoulders. No, I haven't passed my test, I told him. All right, that's better, he said, writing something in his little book and then tearing it out and handing it to me. Take this to your police station with your licence. Right, young man, off you go. Turning to Roothy I heard him say, it's either the bus or you are walking. I whispered to Roothy that I'd pick him up around the corner, and rode away. We were silent all the way home.

It was a Thursday night. I had just walked Jill home, and on the way back I became aware of a car following me. Something told me it was trouble, but I couldn't think of anyone who had it in for me. *Fuck, I've been off the scene for ages; I must be imagining this.* The car suddenly drew level with me and two youths stepped out. One of them

I recognised: it was Vince Clarke. He looked odd getting out of a car with all his motorbike gear on. The other one, who was the driver, I didn't know. Fucking hell, Liz had obviously told Vince that I'd shagged her; that's what this was all about. I thought about legging it. I knew I could outrun them.

My mate here says you've been fucking about with his bird; it was Vince who spoke. I had my back to a wall. Vince came over and leaned against it, lit a cigarette and waited for my answer to his question. My brain was going round in circles; I honestly didn't know what he was on about. I nearly said, don't you mean your bird, Vince. Well, said Vince, have you? I looked at him leaning back on his elbows blowing smoke rings. I don't know what the fuck you're talking about, I said, surprising myself. This response obviously surprised Vince as well; he stopped blowing smoke rings and stood up. I don't even know this cunt, never mind his bird, I said, looking at the other youth for the first time. Vince turned around to him; he was leaning against the car trying to look cool. He says he don't know your bird, and you're a cunt, he laughed. The other one came over, reluctantly I thought. You don't know Jill Brown, you lying bastard, he said, pushing me in the chest. For a moment, at the mention of her name all the fight had gone out of me. If he had hit me then it would have been all over, but he didn't. Instead he looked over at Vince. Vince merely shrugged. He turned back, and I could see fear in his eyes. He swung a weak half-hearted right-hander, which I easily avoided. Grabbing him around the neck, I wrestled him to the ground; he felt weak and limp underneath me. I had never been much of a fighter, and I hesitated with my fist poised above his face. Vince was kneeling at the side of me; I heard the click of his flick knife as it sprang open right before my eyes. Releasing my grip on the youth, our roles were soon reversed, and I found myself with him on top of me. I could have beaten him easily, and I knew he knew it. But with Vince and his flick knife waiting, it had to end this way. Suddenly filled with confidence, he caught me a good one just below my left eye. Fucking stay away from her, he shouted as they drove away.

The next day I stayed off work, not because of my eye, which had turned into a right shiner; I was heartbroken. How could she do this? But had she done anything? It was the longest day of my life; I went from loving her to hating her and back again a thousand times. My dad said I should stick to football instead of women and fighting. It was playing football that did this, I told him, pointing at my eye. He shook his head in disbelief. Somebody caught me with their elbow at training; it was just an accident. Leave him alone, Mum said, coming in from the kitchen; can't you see he's upset? Satisfied with the silence that now prevailed, she went back to the kitchen. I hope you gave him one back, Dad said, putting the evening paper down.

He looked in the direction of the kitchen and leaned towards me. Always make sure you get the first one in, he whispered; hit them in the gut as hard as you can, especially if they've had a few pints. All those times we had got up in the middle of the night to watch Cassius Clay fight came to mind. Thanks Dad, I'll remember that,

I smiled. I didn't tell him I never got any in, never mind the first one. *Ready Steady Go* had started while we were having our little chat; luckily it was only Sonny and Cher. He patted my shoulder and went back to reading the paper. He was all right, my old man. I sat back and waited for The Who to come on. Roothy came around after *Ready Steady Go.* We went outside and sat on the front wall. That's a good un, he said, looking at my eye. I suppose you heard all about it then? I asked him. Yeah: Sue told me. She said Jill's been crying all day. And how the fuck does Jill know any of this? I said angrily. I haven't told her so that leaves her fucking boyfriend. Look, does it matter? She says none of it's true anyway.

She would, wouldn't she? I mean why would this bloke come looking for me if there was no truth in it? I asked him. She says he's been pestering her to go out with him but she keeps telling him no. Do you believe her? I asked him. Yeah I do, he said without hesitating. Nothing could come between you two; you're fucking made for each other. Who the fuck is this bloke anyway? I said, my voice trapped in my throat sounding strange. We were made for each other he had said. I don't know. Roothy looked at his watch and got to his feet. I think they call him Peck or something, but I don't know him. I could have taken the bastard easy, you know, but he had Vince Clarke and a big fucking knife with him. Fuck, you're kidding! Roothy's eyes widened. I'm gonna have to go, he said, looking at his watch again. Are you going round to see her? he asked, turning at the gate. She knows where I am, I told him. I watched him go down the road. If you see her tell her, I shouted after him.

Sitting thinking things over, maybe I had overreacted a little. The thought of her crying was really beginning to get to me. I couldn't stand to see girls cry; it always broke my heart. *Fuck it, I'm going out,* I thought to myself, moping around wasn't doing me any good at all. I put on my favourite Levi's and a white Fred Perry three-button shirt, with my three-quarter-length brown suede coat. I thought about borrowing some of my sister's makeup to hide the yellow bruising around my eye. *Oh fuck it,* I thought, *it makes me look hard.* I had to bump start the scooter down the hill, but it felt good to be riding it again.

Jill's mum said she had gone out, and shut the door. I stood there a minute and then knocked again. She never had liked me, the stuck-up cow. When you say she went out, do you know where exactly? I asked her when she opened the door again. No I don't, but a nice young man called for her. He had a car, she added sarcastically. She shut the door again, obviously my time was up. Thanks a lot cunt, I said aloud. The old fella next door coming up his front path gave me a funny look. How you doing? I smiled at him. He hurried on past, looking over his shoulder.

Well that was it, then. Fuck her, there were plenty more fish in the sea; who the fuck was I kidding? Maybe there was a logical explanation for this. Maybe it was all just a misunderstanding; but for the life of me, I couldn't think of one. The Derwent Social Club was packed. Big Trev was on the door. I asked him if Roothy was in. Yeah, he's here, he shouted above the music; well, at least he *was*, I ain't seen him leave. It was five bob to get in; Trev stamped my wrist and let me in for nothing.

Standing just inside the door, trying to adjust my eyes to the flashing pink and blue lights. After a couple of minutes I caught sight of Sue dancing with a crowd of girls. I knew Roothy wouldn't be dancing; he only danced when he was pissed, and it was too early yet. Pushing my way through to the bar, *This Old Heart of Mine* by the Isley Brothers came on the turntable, and the dancefloor became even more crowded. Roothy was propping up the bar, a half-drunk pint in front of him. I didn't think you were bothering, he said, leaning over and shouting in my ear. Fuck it, spilt milk and all that, I shrugged. He smiled, what you having? Put your money away, I'll get these, I told him. Sue came over, out of breath and slightly perspiring, her nipples hard beneath her top. She looked really shagable. Looking at another girl like that, it saddened me that I was thinking it was all over. I bent down close and asked her what she wanted to drink.

She shook her head no. Come outside, she said, pulling my arm. Whew, that's better. You can't hear yourself think in there. She ran her fingers through her hair and leaned against the railings. She really loves you, you know, she said, looking right into my eyes. So everyone keeps telling me, but she's got a funny way of showing it, I smiled. Are you listening to me? I heard her say. She reached out and tenderly touched my black eye. Does it hurt? she asked. No, my eyes are fine, it's this that hurts. I put my hand across my heart. It's broken. She smiled. That's better, she said. I knew at that moment she wouldn't stay with Roothy, she was too good for him. He was my best friend but he was turning into a pisshead, and when he was drunk he was dangerous. The door opened and The Who's *It's Not True* spilled into the warm night air. At last, a decent fucking record, I said. Sometimes, Jonty, I don't understand you. She looked serious. Do you know she's gone out with him tonight? I asked her. Yes she said, but it's not what you think. Yeah right, I shrugged. She agreed to go out with him so she could tell him she's not interested, and to please her mum, she added. I might have known that fucking bitch had something to do with it, I laughed. Don't worry, it's you she loves; this time tomorrow you two will be back together. Come on, let's go back inside; she took hold of my hand. You're too good-looking, you know that don't you? she smiled. You're really pretty. Fucking pretty, I laughed. Nothing wrong with pretty, she said. No, there wasn't.

Saturday afternoon I spent the whole of the match looking for Jill; she never showed and neither did Roothy. It was fucking crap and we lost. Sitting at home that night feeling sorry for myself, I picked up the green un and started to memorise the football results. Ever since I had been able to read I could tell anyone who cared to listen every result and even the half-time score of every match in all four divisions and even the Scottish leagues. *What a sad twat,* I thought, throwing the paper on the table and getting up. What's the matter with you? Mum asked. Is it Jill again? I ignored her and went upstairs. This just wasn't right, a seventeen-year-old boy with no girlfriend and no friends, staying in on a Saturday night? I washed my hair and borrowed my sister's hairdryer. *Fucking hell, I was pretty*, I thought, looking in the mirror, remembering what Sue had said.

The navy blue suit fitted me like a second skin, and walking down the road I started to feel good again. There was quite a crowd waiting at the bus station, and everyone seemed to be with someone; one or two of them were familiar, but I didn't really know them. Maybe this wasn't such a good idea after all. I felt like a spare prick at a wedding. Going back home seemed the best option, when Ronnie and Phil, two lads I had gone to school with, came around the corner. Normally I wouldn't have been seen dead with these two; nothing against them, they were okay. They were sort of like pretend Mods, not the real thing. But at that moment I was just glad to see a friendly face, and my snobbery was forgotten. I bummed a fag off Ronnie; one wasn't going to hurt. You going into town, Jonty? Phil asked. Yeah, I'm meeting this bird, I lied. They looked at each other, and I knew what they were thinking: what about Jill? So where you two off to? I asked them, avoiding the awkwardness. I don't know, Ronnie said, more than likely Clouds; they have some good groups on there. The bus came, and as we filed on I said, Fuck the bird, I might come with you two. I think I made their night: the fucking ace Mod on the town with them. The night turned out pretty good; the only downside was listening to fucking Soul music all night.

The only downside of being a Mod was pretending to like that Soul shit, or maybe it was just me. Ronnie and Phil turned out to be pretty good company, and after a few pints and a handful of fuck knows what pills, bought from some cockney ponce, I was buzzing again. The place was teeming with girls, and I even had a few dances. But not even the beer and pills could get Jill out of my mind.

Waiting for the last bus home, I saw Liz Walters snogging some old Ted; his mate was hanging around, obviously pissed off because he hadn't pulled. He must have seen me looking at them. Hey Dob, there's another one of them Mod puffs over here, he shouted. Dob showed no interest, thank fuck. The other one started to come across.Ronnie and Phil were standing nearby. Fuck, they were Mods; *go and pick on them, cunt,* I thought, trying to look inconspicuous. He started to walk away, then he turned around again, never make eye contact, but I did. What the fuck are you looking at, you ponce? he said, covering me in spit.

He grabbed hold of the front of my shirt, and put his face right next to mine. How about it? his words slurred out on his beer breath, come on, just you and me. Over his shoulder I could see that Dob was starting to show a bit of interest. Fucking leave him alone, Danny, he shouted; he's only a fucking kid. For fuck's sake, you've only just come out; do you want to go down again? Danny was having trouble standing in the same spot; he was swaying all over the place. He half-turned to look for his mate. What my dad had said, about hitting them in the gut if they had been drinking, came to mind at that very moment.

Danny had missed his chance, and I didn't want another black eye. I hit him as hard as I could in the midriff. He let out a loud gasp of air and stared at me in disbelief before crumpling to the floor in a heap. Kneeling down over him, I cracked him at the side of his ear. Hey cunt, do you want some as well? I shouted at Dob, getting to my feet and moving towards him. He unwrapped himself from Liz and started to walk away. It's nothing to do with me, mate, he called over his shoulder. Behind me, Danny was on his knees throwing up. Just for a brief moment I had a vision of myself as some mean, bitter, twisted fuck, someone always looking for a fight; in reality nothing could be further from the truth. I became aware all around of everyone watching; it had all happened so fast.

On the bus going home I could feel a change towards me, respect for all the wrong reasons. It didn't make me feel any better; in fact, I felt sorry for Danny puking on the floor, and worse, I felt sorry for myself. Liz, showing no loyalty to the bloke she'd just been snogging, walked up home with me, her arm in mine again; it was almost déjà vu. What happened to Vince? I asked her. What happened to Jill? she replied.

Chapter Four

Monday morning, when dad shook me awake, I told him I was coming down with something, and I was going to stay in bed. He never even argued, and when I heard him shut the door, the thought that he had given up on me was an awful realisation. When I eventually got up I wished I had gone to work, but it was too late. I took the scooter out for a spin and spent an hour browsing in Fowlers record shop.

On the way back past my old school, it was dinnertime, the kids hanging about in the playground and outside the school gates. Pulling up across the road, I thought about what old Jake had said on my last day at school. We had gone around smashing every milk bottle we could find, which seemed really childish now. Schooldays are the best days of your life. You might laugh now, he said to our response, but within a few months you will wish you were back here. *The old bastard was right*, I thought, as I watched with envy. All these carefree kids; it seemed such a long time ago that I had been one of them; in reality it was only a year.

A couple of girls who had been in my class walked by, a right pair of swots, I used to think, because they chose to stay on. Stuck up bitches, I said to myself, as they never acknowledged me. Just at that moment they stopped and turned around. Hello, she said, coming back smiling. Her name was Diane Taylor, and God was she fit. I thought you were ignoring me, I smiled at her. Her friend started giggling.

She's not wearing her glasses, she explained; she didn't see you. Well, put them on; you might be talking to a lamppost or something. Diane put them on, laughing; she looked even more attractive. They really suit you, I told her; you look lovely. She blushed ever so slightly, and looked down at the floor. She reached out and ran her hand along the chrome backrest. I like your scooter, she said. Hop on the back, and I'll give you a lift across the road to school. She smiled her lovely smile again. I patted the back seat; I'm being serious, jump on. Diane climbed on the back. Hold on, I told her, and I felt her arms around my waist. We drove through the school gates and into the playground.

All the kids stopped and stared, it was a wonderful moment, until Jake suddenly appeared from nowhere. What do you think you are playing at? he shouted; get that thing out of here before I call the police! Diane got off the back. Diane Taylor, I must say I'm surprised at you and a little disappointed, Jake admonished her. I revved the scooter and turned around. Sorry, I mouthed to Diane and winked at her. Jake turned his attention to me for the first time. You, young man, are sadly no surprise. Sir, you were right, and I apologise, I told him and rode away.

Friday night, me, Roothy and Sue went to the Pot Hole. I didn't really like playing gooseberry, but it was better than going out on my own. I convinced myself I was over Jill, but all the way there all I did was ask Sue about her. Actually, it had been my idea to come here; I was hoping to see Diane. I'd heard this was where she hung out on Friday nights. Roothy didn't know it was soft drinks only or he wouldn't have come. It was a red-hot night, and the place was packed. After about half an hour and no sign of Diane, Roothy and me went to the pub across the road. Speed and barley wine were a lethal combination.

Andy Bailey was sitting over in the corner of the bar, so we went over to say hello. He had this bird with him; she looked quite a bit older than him, but she wasn't half good looking. Not many people liked Andy; they thought he was a weirdo and a bigheaded twat. Me, I thought he was fucking ace, always one step a head of everyone else. Andy called everyone 'man', and carried books with him everywhere he went in a BOAC shoulder bag. He was reading the *Big Sur* and ignoring the bird. He folded a corner of the page he was reading and closed the book when we sat down. Since the last time I had seen him he had grown a moustache, a real droopy one; he looked fucking cool. Long time no see, Andy, I greeted him. How you doin? Jonty man. I just got back from the smoke, he said. The bird smirked and Andy ignored her.

I put the plastic bag of purple hearts on the table. Thanks man, Andy said, taking a couple. Can I have some? the bird asked me. Help yourself, I told her, really looking at her for the first time. She had long, really black hair, which hung across her face in a really sexy way. She stood up and held out her hand. Anyone got change for the jukebox? I handed her two tanners, and she gave me a come-on smile. She was wearing a black and white mini skirt, and her legs seemed to go on forever as she walked across the room.

Andy got out a little red tin from his bag and lit a joint. Man, this is good shit, he said, passing it round. Fuck, he wasn't wrong. The sweet smell of the grass hung on my senses; I started to giggle at the thought of the whole pub getting stoned. What's so funny? The bird said, coming back to the table. Otis Redding was singing *I Can't Turn You Loose*. Did you put this fucking shit on, Glenda? Andy said getting to his feet. I watched him as though I were dreaming; he seemed to be floating. Soon The Who had replaced Otis Redding. Substitute me for him. Glenda was sitting next to me, talking in my ear; she told me she was a nurse; her breath was warm and sweet. Across the table Roothy was talking, his mouth opening and closing, but nothing was coming out. Our little corner of the world drifted in and out of a stony haze for the rest of the night.

Leaving with Glenda on my arm I saw a vision of a sweet beautiful girl wearing glasses. For a moment I remembered the reason I was there. The beautiful girl looked sad when our eyes met, I felt like crying for her sadness, but I could not remember her name. Waiting at the bus stop, Glenda had her tongue down my throat and her hand rubbing my crotch. I pushed her away as I remembered the name of the girl with the glasses: Diane Taylor. But it wasn't her who made me push the nurse away, it was Jill, but Glenda wasn't easily put off.

On the top deck of the bus she had my dick out. Glenda dragged me off the bus at her stop, which meant a long walk home for me. She pulled me behind a hedge, and soon we were fucking in someone's front garden, with people walking past just a few feet away. Upstairs in the house, lights came on, while she fucked me stupid. I had never known a girl like this; it was certainly true what they said about nurses. We arranged to meet the following night and shared the longest kiss goodnight. The walk home gave me time to think; my head was clearing, the plastic bag in my pocket empty. The trouble with thinking, was thinking did me no good at all; the direction my life was taking was no direction at all. Fuck it, it had been a brilliant night, I kidded myself.

When I got back to our shithole of a little town, I needed to be careful; Mods were still in the minority. There were still one or two drunken Teds and Greabos knocking around. I was getting through quite nicely when I saw someone walking towards me. As he got nearer I recognised him: it was Vince's mate from the other week, the one who had given me a shiner, the one who had caused me and Jill to split up. He must have recognised me at the same time. He stopped. Listen, about the other week, you know, me hitting you. Well, fuck it, you can have her, he said, as though he was doing me a favour. The cunt obviously didn't get it; there was no Vince this time, no menacing flick knife, just him and me, the new hard man. Was he fucking stupid or what? Didn't he know I let him hit me? Where's the motor? I asked him. It's my dad's, he said, as though we were the best of friends. I cracked him a good one straight in the mouth.

He sat on his arse in the gutter, his bottom lip pissing blood. Looking down at him I saw the fear in his eyes. I had been there, and I would go there again, but now I had learned how to hide that fear, a dangerous thing. Walking away without a word, I felt bad, I felt ashamed; hitting people was not the answer. At the same time there was joy and elation, that Jill would be mine again. I headed straight to Jill's house, safe in the knowledge, at least in my mind, that we were where we were meant to be.

The house was in darkness when I arrived; I went silently down the side and through the gate. A light was still on in her room. Searching around for something to throw at the window, I remembered all the fruit trees and bushes at the top of the garden. Armed with a handful of gooseberries I gently aimed one at her window. On the third throw she opened the window. Jill, it's me, I said from the darkness. SHH! she laughed, leaning out of her bedroom window. A minute later she opened the back door. Quietly closing it behind her, she draped her arms around my neck and drew me close. I'm sorry. I'm so sorry, she sobbed, her tears warm on my skin. I pulled her face up to look at me; we kissed like only we could kiss. The moon appeared between the houses; there was no bigger moment, there never would be. The moonlight shone through her nightdress, her pale transparent beauty lay beneath my hands. I love you, I heard her say, and all the time we looked into each other's eyes.

Why? Why did you have to hit him? Jill had noticed my grazed knuckles and the dried blood. He hit me first, Jill, remember. She didn't seem to hear me. The moment had gone just like the moon. But the moon would soon be back. What does it matter, Jill? I promise no more fighting. What if I'm pregnant? she said, pushing herself away from me. Don't be stupid. Of course you won't get pregnant. Why? Did I imagine what we just did? she said sarcastically. She opened the back door. I've got to go, she said. Jill, it's the middle of the night; you don't have to go anywhere. Sshh, keep your voice down, she pleaded. Sorry, I said, pulling her towards me. I kissed her, and for that moment, we were together again. Tomorrow, where will I meet you, I said as she started to close the door. No, I can't, she said; it's too soon. Fuck, I don't believe this, I started to say, but she had shut the door.

All night I lay awake and wondered if it had all been a dream. It was real, all right, it was real that we had made love under the moonlight, it was real that she had said I Love You. It was also real that I hadn't said a prayer to God: Don't let Jill be pregnant. I really didn't care; I hoped she was. Just leave her alone for a couple of days, let her sort out her head, I decided. When at last I fell asleep it was in the certain knowledge that we were meant to be together, and nothing would come between us except death.

Saturday afternoon, I couldn't wait any longer. I took the scooter out and rode up to Jill's. About fifty yards from her house, I saw them come out together and get into daddy's car. They drove away, and I sat and watched. I watched for a long time, then I went home.

Glenda had no conversation; all she wanted to do was shag. We had been going out for almost a month, seeing each other three or four times a week. All we did was fuck, which was great for a while. Maybe it was me – well, I know it was me; all I did when we were together was think of Jill. One Saturday night at the Pavilion, where we had gone to see Geno Washington, Glenda spent most of the night talking to her ex-boyfriend. She kept giving me 'what are you going to do about it' looks. But I was looking for a way out, and he was doing me a favour.

Tommy was there with a group of Mods who I vaguely knew but didn't like. They were all rich kids; mummy and daddy bought them everything. They were all going down the motorway to the twenty-four-hour services for breakfast, so I tagged along. Outside, Glenda and her ex were snogging passionately. I smiled to myself. Glenda would be better off without me. There were two cars full of us. I found myself in the back seat of one car with three birds and a lad. One of the girls was sitting on my knee, and I was starting to come down into this wonderful mellow feeling. These kids were not so bad after all, and even the breakfast tasted good.

Chapter Five

Suddenly I was moving in different circles, and I had hardly seen anything of Roothy. I know he didn't care much for the company I was keeping – maybe he was right – I know he was right. But for now I had nothing better, and the pills were free and plentiful. The main reason I stuck around was this girl called Viv. She lived in this fucking big house, almost a mansion, but she had no airs and graces, she was just a really nice girl. The trouble was she had a boyfriend, a right poser called Kenny. He had all the clothes, clothes to die for, but he just didn't have the style to carry them off; he was a fucking fake. Because they all lived in big houses, I always got them to drop me off or pick me up well away from our house.That really bothered me; I was ashamed of being ashamed of where I lived. And then there was my dad; I remember the first time I took Jill back to ours. Mum was all right, but Dad always walked around the house in his vest and drank tea from the biggest fucking mug you had ever seen. Both his arms were tattooed from his time in the navy, and he rolled his own fags sitting in his chair licking the paper.

The sound of a car horn outside had my mum peeping through the curtains; it couldn't be for us; we didn't know anyone with a car. It looks like some friends of yours, she said, pulling the curtain wider to get a better view. I got up and looked over her shoulder; Viv was coming through our front gate. Mum, get away from the window, I said, pulling her arm. Stop gawping. I was frantically pulling on my desert boots, wondering who the fuck had told them where the fuck I lived. Dad came in with a mug of tea; where's the fire? I heard him say as I closed the door behind me.

They were going to a party, and wondered if I wanted to come, Viv explained as I led her back down our front path, still tucking my shirt in and with my bootlaces flapping. She never mentioned anything about knowing where I lived so I didn't ask. Things were looking up; Kenny the poser wasn't with her. The party was in some huge mock Tudor mansion out in the country. The hallway was bigger than the whole of our house, with carpet so deep it felt like I was sinking. The bird who was holding the party made everyone take their shoes off. Fuck that, I knew I had holes in my socks. I told her my religion wouldn't allow me to take my shoes off in public. She looked at me a bit funny, until Viv told her it was true. I think she really believed us, she even said sorry. It felt really nice to have Viv holding on to my arm laughing and joking; she thought I was really witty and clever. We sat halfway up the stairs, laughing at some young lads dancing like spastics to some Soul shit. It occurred to me that all my new acquaintances – I wouldn't call them friends – didn't work; they were either at college or still at school.

I was probably the only one there who worked for a living. *Fuck it,* I thought, *why couldn't I do that*? Viv had told me I was clever, but it was just another passing fantasy. If I packed up work there would be no money for clothes, for my scooter, and a car, which I desperately wanted. I didn't have no rich mummy and daddy to support me. We found an empty bedroom and lay on the bed kissing; she was happy to let me play with her tits, but I knew she wouldn't let me go any further. She hadn't turned me down, but she had a boyfriend, and I wasn't going to try. We both knew we had different futures mapped out, but I liked her company and she liked mine.

Sometimes though it seemed almost like *Lady Chatterley's Lover*: I was her bit of rough. Or was she my bit of posh? Have you ever read *Lady Chatterley's Lover*? I asked her. No, she said, peering at me closely to see if I was kidding or being serious. Have you? Not really, just skipped through it looking for the dirty bits. She laughed. I don't really like Lawrence; I prefer Steinbeck. Does Kenny know? I asked her, looking serious. She looked at me for a moment and then cracked up laughing. Very funny, she said, pulling me towards her. The realisation that Viv would probably end up living in a house like this, probably even with Kenny, *God I hope not*, brought me back to what Roothy said: rich cunts.

We went downstairs, and while Viv got talking to her mates, I wandered around the house. They were richer than I thought: I had never seen so many rooms. A table laden with all sorts of food was in the centre of one of the rooms. I found a plastic bag and filled it with fancy looking things for my mum to try: she loved anything like that.

The DJ lived not far from me, and it was nice to see a familiar face, and we got talking about records. There was this blonde bird hanging around, and after a while the DJ asked me if I would take over from him for half an hour. I reckon I'm on a promise, he said, looking at the blonde. He'd got two turntables and hundreds of records all neatly stacked in boxes. I was in heaven; I've got this thing about records. To me all the different coloured sleeves and labels were like diamonds.

If I ever went to anyone's house, the first thing I did was seek out their record collection. You could find out all you needed to know about people by what was in their record collection. Midnight Hour was playing, and The Bar-Kays were waiting on the other turntable. I changed it to the Small Faces, *All Or Nothing*. Fucking hell, it was like finding a treasure chest, as I picked out some great records to play. *It's All Over Now* by the Valentinos, *Five O'clock World* by The Vogues – Jesus, I couldn't believe my luck, he had a fucking copy of *Jump and Dance* by The Carnaby. It was Jill's favourite record. I'd never seen a copy before. By the time the DJ got back from shagging the blonde, I had about a dozen rare records hidden in my coat.

The bloke who drove us to the party was called Stewart, and he was a bit of a nutter behind the wheel of a car. His car was a black souped-up Austin 1100 with spacers and a tiny racing steering wheel. Stewart wore black leather driving gloves and drove like a bat out of hell. When we all piled back into his car at the end of the night, we had acquired two more passengers, and Stewart had been popping pills all night like the rest of us, and even in my fuzzed up mind, a brief thought appeared that he shouldn't be driving. Just for a moment I considered getting out, but it was a long walk home. Looking at all the faces in the car, there was no concern on any of them. It was me just thinking too much again. There were five of us in the back and three in the front. Viv was sitting on my lap, squashed into the corner; the others in the back I didn't know at all. Stewart's bird Allison and his best mate, a lad called Chris, who I knew quite well, were sitting in the front. Stewart still managed to get some speed out of the car despite the extra weight. Everyone was high, and the feeling of foreboding I had began to fade.

Chris was out of his head in the front; he kept asking Stewart to pull over so he could throw up. Stewart ignored him so he wound down the window and stuck his head out. The fresh air seemed to do him good; after a while he started yelling at people walking in the streets. Everyone was laughing at him, which encouraged him to do it even more. He kept leaning further and further out, and all the while Allison was trying to pull him back. I fucking love you, he yelled at two birds in mini skirts, and that was the last thing he ever said. The sound was horrible, like no other sound I had ever heard, but I knew instantly what it was. We were probably doing fifty when his head hit the tree. I think if Allison had not got hold of him, the impact would have dragged him through the window.

Instead he slumped back down in the seat, what was left of his head, a bloody pulp hanging at a crazy angle, his neck broken. Allison let out a piercing scream, and Stewart brought the car to a shuddering halt. What the fuck's the matter with you, he shouted at her, and then he saw it. Stewart jumped out of the car and ran across the road before sinking to his knees and throwing up. Everyone in the back was fighting to get out, I managed to push the driver's seat forward, and we all got out. I went around to the passenger's side. Allison wouldn't move, she was frozen with fear. Chris looked like he was asleep, his face untouched. Looking back down the road at the tree where I knew the back of his head was, he let out a pitiful gasp of breath, almost like a sigh, that made me jump back. Inside the car Allison started to scream again. A man in a suit knelt by the side of me and leaned inside the car. There's nothing you can do for him, son, he said gravely, covering Chris with his jacket.

A crowd of people had begun to gather around. I wanted to shout at them, tell them to go away, but the words would not come, stuck in my dry throat. Death was all around; it hung heavily on the night air and everyone present for that moment knew their fate. Allison was still sitting there, her screams replaced by wracking sobs. The cops arrived, reluctantly followed a minute later by an ambulance, its tired siren struggling to be heard. I moved away from the car and sat on the pavement edge wondering if Chris was floating above, watching this eerie flashing neon scene. As I turned my head to look up at the starlit heavens, they sunk a needle into Allison's arm. Viv came and sat beside me. I looked at her tear-stained face. She was looking for an answer, for a reason – I had neither.

I put my arm around her shoulder and pulled her closer. Viv, lovely sweet Viv, she should not have seen this.

It's funny how you find yourself something of a celebrity, when people find out you were at the scene of something fatal. As word of Chris' death got around, so the truth of what happened became twisted and distorted. Why do people want to talk so much about death? Viv sought comfort back in the arms of Kenny. For a long time I felt I needed to talk to her, to tell her what I didn't say that fateful night. Gradually the feeling faded; it was too late now anyway. Mick's funeral had been hard enough, and even though I had liked Chris I had no intention of going to another one. Instead I said a silent prayer for him, me the non-believer. It was something I always did after I had shagged some bird without protection. Please God, I'll do anything, even go to church, but please don't let her be pregnant. Life goes on without the dead, and soon it would be hard to even remember Chris as he faded from our thoughts just like the mark on the tree.

Chapter Six

Roothy and Sue had finished, just like I knew they would. He was fast turning into an alcoholic, and just for a while she was heading the same way. August Bank Holiday found us both free and single, leaning on the front door of the Duke, waiting for the doors to open at midday. Eighteen and single, we should have been on top of the world, but the world was shit, at least mine was. Every night waiting for the pub to open, drinking and playing table football, Roothy said he wasn't bothered about Sue, but all he did was talk about her. All I did was think about Jill; I just could not get her out of my mind. There seemed to be nothing I could do to help myself, stuck in a bottomless pit of self-pity.

One Saturday night in the Duke, we heard about a party somewhere. Word soon spread, and we piled into the back of someone's van, not even knowing where we were going. Soon the van was full, and I found myself with a girl sitting on my lap. We started kissing, and she was obviously high. I slipped my hand inside her blouse, and she didn't stop me. Reaching down with my other hand to get up her skirt, I found someone had beaten me to it. It was Roothy, the bastard. The thought of kissing her while someone else played with her cunt turned me right off. The fucking slag, he could have her.

There were loads at the party spilling out of the front door into the garden; they didn't seem to mind a few more. I grabbed a beer and began to pick my way through all the sweating bodies, in the hope that Jill might be there. Across the room I spotted Diane; she saw me at the same time. I smiled at her, and she waved back hesitantly. I had let my hair grow longer since the last time I had seen her, trying to copy Steve Marriott. Hi, she said, smiling brightly. She reached out her hand and touched my hair. It suits you, she said. It looks really nice.

Diane had that way about her, so young, yet so mature. She had her long hair tied back in a ponytail, and she was wearing her glasses. Glad to see you're wearing your glasses, or you would never have seen me, I said, leaning close to make myself heard. Someone was playing *A Legal Matter* over and over again at full volume; I looked around to see who it was. I couldn't even see the record player. Whoever it was had great taste. Boys don't make passes at girls who wear glasses, she said seriously. I dropped down on one knee in front of her: Will you marry me? I asked, her, taking her hand. You're mad, she said, laughing. We're all mad, just take a look around. Everyone in the room seemed to be singing It's A Legal Matter, baby. She pulled me to my feet. You shouldn't joke about things like that, she said. Boys do make passes at girls who wear glasses; I winked at her and pulled her close to kiss her. Well, will you? I asked her, our lips still almost touching after the sweetest kiss. Right at this moment probably yes, she whispered. Is that it? That is not an answer. Each time we spoke our lips touched like tiny kisses. Yes, the answer is definitely yes, her words forming on my lips. We found somewhere to sit and talked for hours. She was unlike any girl I had ever known before. I had always thought of myself as quite intelligent; after all, I did read loads of books. All that intelligence had been wasted on other girls, but with Diane I just couldn't stop talking. Although, a lack of intelligence ended the night. I'd gone to get us a drink when Roothy called me over; he was sitting on the sofa with this fat bird with long greasy hair. He had his hand up her sweater playing with her tits; I could see his thinking, they were enormous. Behind the sofa was a table full of food, with a birthday cake in the middle. I don't know what made me do it – just a silly impulse. There were about thirty or so little paper dishes filled with trifle; someone had really gone to a lot of trouble. Picking up one of the dishes I pushed it into Roothy's face. You cunt, he said, getting to his feet spitting trifle. He reached behind the sofa for another dish and did the same to me, a huge grin on his face. Pretty soon nearly everyone had joined in a massive trifle fight. The girl whose party it was stood in the middle of the room crying; even her birthday cake had been thrown. What had seemed funny just a few minutes ago now seemed stupid and childish. The party was over and everyone drifted away. I persuaded Roothy to stay and help me clear up. It took us more than an hour; the girl couldn't thank us enough, and Diane thought how kind and considerate I was. I couldn't bring myself to tell them the truth, that it was my fault entirely.

We began seeing each other; Diane was good for me at a really bad time. I found I no longer needed the drink and the drugs, and I was thinking about going to night school – me the responsible adult. I started driving lessons and began saving for a car. For the first time since we split up, I found I was no longer constantly thinking about Jill. The ironic thing was that thinking about forgetting her brought her right back into my thoughts. All that I had with Diane I knew I would give up for Jill. I was waiting across the road from the bus stop, for the number ninety-two to drop Diane off. Catching my reflection in the glass of a shop window, I turned to look at myself. I was fooling no one; fuck it, I knew what I had to do. Are you into handbags, or were you admiring yourself? a voice said at my side. Sue stood there, another girl with her. Caught me out. Which one would suit me? I smiled.

Have you heard? she said, sounding excited. The look on her face told me she knew I hadn't. It's all over, she blurted out, without waiting for me to ask what was all over. She could have meant the world was over or life as we know it was over. I stared at her blankly, but I knew what she meant. They were both chewing gum and looking at me intently. All I was aware of was their mouths moving silently. Sue's friend blew a bubble, and the popping noise it made when it burst brought me back to focus. You're telling me she's finished with him. At last, Sue rolled her eyes; yeah, she's finished with him. So, what do you want me to do? I knew you'd say that, she laughed. The other girl started to laugh as well. I fixed her a stare and she stopped. What the hell had any of this got to do with her anyway? Come on, Sue, are we going? she said, spitting out her gum. I looked at her, seeing her for the first time; she seemed close to tears, and I wished I hadn't upset her. You know what, Jonty, you're not worth bothering with, Sue said, turning to catch up with her friend. Jill's better off without you, she added as a parting shot. She caught up with her friend and slipped her arm through hers. Jesus, how can they get away with that, I thought to myself. Girls arm in arm with each other really did something to me. Don't take any notice of him, Moira, Sue said in a loud voice; he's a prick. Moira – that was a nice name. Sorry, Moira, I didn't mean to upset you, I called after them. Yeah, I love you too, I said to myself when they chose to ignore me.

Diane stepped off the bus, her lovely smile spreading only goodness – all for me, the bastard who knew what was coming. The night was fucking torture, but it made me realise I had been headed in the wrong direction. She knew it was all over, the moment I didn't return her smile when she stepped off the bus. I don't understand, she said as we waited for her last bus home. I could have told her about destiny, something Jill and me had talked about. It could not be changed; we were always going to end up together no matter what. Instead I just shrugged my shoulders. You don't have to wait, she said. No it's okay, I want to, I told her. Please, I'd sooner you went; there's nothing more to say. So I walked away, just fucking walked away. She was right, she didn't understand, she never would, unless she was ever lucky enough to love someone so much the pain was unbearable.

Was it only a week ago that me and Jill had been sitting in the Queen's Head having a quiet drink? Just us two, three old blokes playing dominoes, Reggie the mad glass collector, the landlord and his pet mynah bird. Roothy had spent hours teaching the bird to say fuck off, which it did to everyone who walked past its cage on the corner of the bar. Oh, we were back together all right; in fact, Jill clung to me as though her life depended on it, telling me again and again how much she had missed me, how sorry she was. She looked more like Carol White than ever, in fact Carol didn't even come close. We were holding hands across the table; fuck was I a lucky bastard. What are you thinking about, Jonty? she said, squeezing my hand. Wouldn't you like to know, I smiled. Are you going to go and get what we came in for? she whispered, leaning across to kiss me. What we had come in for was to get a packet of Durex from the machine in the gents'.

Suddenly the door flew open, and there must have been about twenty Rockers piling in. Fucking hell, that was all I needed. Luckily I knew four or five of them, who I had gone to school with. There was a lad called Nellie who had been one of my best mates at school. I hadn't seen him for ages. He came over and sat down. He was dripping wet. All right, Jonty, he said, smiling at Jill. Don't look so worried, we're not looking for any trouble. Thanks, Nellie, I smiled, wishing I was as confident as him. Is it raining? I asked him. No, why? He looked puzzled. You're fucking soaking man. He laughed. Piss, he said. Piss, I repeated, parrot fashion. Yeah, it's a greaser thing, a sort of initiation. You're not a true greaser until everyone's pissed on you. Jill pulled a face. That's disgusting.

What is? someone said, pulling up a chair and sitting down. I recognised him straight away – fucking Bob Jackson. Bob was a sort of legend around town, the hardest bastard there was. I took a sneaky glance at him; he was older than all the rest of them, in fact a lot older. He looked more like an old Teddy boy than a greaser. Someone handed him a pint, and I noticed the tattooed letters across the back of his knuckles. So who's the puff? he said, turning to look at me. He's all right, Bob, Nellie told him. Jonty's a good mate. Bob had already lost interest in me and was busy chatting up Jill. I finished my drink and kicked Jill's foot under the table. Well, we've got to get off, I said, pushing the chair back and standing up. What, already? Bob said. What's the matter? Don't you like our company? No it's just that we have a bus to catch, I stammered. Well, don't let me stop you, pretty boy. It must be well past your bedtime, he sneered. All the others laughed like crazy at his little joke. All this time he was looking at Jill, her dark eyes filled with fear. For a split second as I stood over him I thought about hitting him; after all, wasn't I a fucking hard man too? Instead I took hold of Jill's hand and pulled her to her feet. At that moment I realised that I hadn't got my jacket. Jesus, it was on the back of the chair Bob was sitting on and he was leaning back against it. For a moment I thought about leaving it. Fuck it, it was my favourite a white cord Levi; I wasn't leaving that. As we walked past I tugged it neatly from under him and didn't look back. Even the mynah bird had the sense to keep quiet.

Outside I looked at Jill and said, Fucking run. We ran like the wind, until we could run no more, then we ducked into a channel and peered cautiously back the way we had come. There was no sight or sound of them. I think we got away with it, I said, leaning back against the wall. We looked at one another and started to laugh. On that cold, damp night, our bodies warm from running and laughing, we made love right there up against the wall. With the money for the machine still in my pocket, as though it was meant to be, the best day of my life so far.

Things were changing fast, very fast, and not for the better. The good times seemed to be running out. What a fucking twat – I gave it all up for Jill. The pathetic thing is, I know I would do it all again. One week, just one fucking week. She had taken me for a ride, used me to get back with her asshole of a fucking boyfriend.

I'm sitting at home contemplating fucking nothing. You're not staying in again? Mum asked. She was reading *Rebecca* again for the hundredth time. It's still the same ending as last time, I said, giving her a dirty look. There's plenty more fish in the sea, she carried on. God, if she says that one more time I'll fucking throttle her. Stop feeling sorry for yourself and get off out. What about that nice young girl, the one with the car? she persisted. It wasn't her car. What wasn't hers? she said, standing in front of me. Do you mind I'm trying to watch this, I said moving my head from side to side with exaggerated movements. No you're not, you're just sulking. Anyway, your dad's programme is on in a minute, she said, changing channels. Oh fuck it, I said under my breath, getting up and going upstairs. When I came back down I was changed and ready to go out; I just couldn't stay in. Fuck it, nobody stayed in on a Saturday night, even if I just walked the streets for a couple of hours. Mum never said a word; Dad was fast asleep on the sofa. So much for his favourite programme. I banged the door shut behind me on the way out.

Realising I didn't know where I was going, I stood outside our front gate like a man with amnesia. Fuck, everyone knew where they were going when they stepped outside their front door. What a sad fucker I was: no girlfriend, even worse no friends. Roothy was my best mate, but I hadn't seen him for ages. I thought about going to look for him, but he might be going out with someone by now. I decided to head into town and maybe just blend in. It was better than walking deserted streets and thinking about Jill. A kind of panic had begun to grip me over the past few days. What if I never met anyone? What if I ended up on the fucking shelf? Fucking hell, I was beginning to sound more like a girl every day.

Going past the Duke, looking through the windows, I could see it was packed to the rafters. Pausing for a moment I thought about going in; no one would notice I was on my own in that crowd. While I was weighing up the situation, a couple of lads came out whom I knew slightly. The noise following them from the open door was deafening, the smell of beer, smoke and perfume intoxicating. Hey Jonty, they greeted me, coming over. They had a couple of birds with them, both of them dressed the same in maroon full-length leather coats. They looked like a couple of right slags. Heard about what you did to that fucking Teddy boy. Fucking ace, man, one of them said. Why, what happened? said the slightly blonder of the two girls. He kicked the shit out of some fucking Ted, he told her proudly. Really? she said, giving me a sort of coy look from under her fringe. Actually, up close she wasn't that bad looking. She must have been the other lad's bird because he put his arm around her shoulder, as though I was some kind of threat. See you, Jonty, they said, turning to go. Yeah see you, I replied, still trying to remember their names. I watched them go, the lad still holding on to Blondie. If I had had a bird on my arm, things would have been different. I might as well have 'on the pull' written on my fucking forehead.

And what was all that shit about the Teddy boy? I hadn't enjoyed hitting him, even though he'd asked for it. Suddenly people were looking at me differently: Jonty the fucking hard man. I laughed at myself; that was total bollocks. Shit, was it only a matter of time before people were queuing up to pick a fight with me. The fastest gunslinger trapped in a town full of trigger-happy cowboys. Deciding against the Duke, and vowing to become a pacifist, I headed back the way I had come.

Jonty, someone shouted from across the road. I stopped and looked. Omo came over wearing his black and white Derby scarf. Don't you ever learn? I asked him; what was it? three nil. We were fucking robbed? Well no, really we were fucking shite, he laughed. We walked along putting the world to rights. Are you coming in for one? Omo asked me as we passed the Midland Hotel. It was the best offer I had had: the only offer. How did you get on today? he asked me as we stood at the bar. I don't know, I didn't play. How come? They never dropped you, did they? He looked surprised. Did they fuck. I told them I was injured. I can't be bothered with football at the moment. You're a fucking idiot, he said, shaking his head. When's this trial with Notts. County? he asked after a while. It was months ago. He waited for me to continue. Don't tell me you didn't go? he said at my silence. I shrugged my shoulders. There's a lot happening right now you know. Jesus fucking Christ, I don't believe you. Do you want to carry on working in that shithole foundry? That was a chance to get out. What are you, my fucking dad? I laughed, making a joke of it. It's your round, dad, I said, holding out my empty glass.

After a couple of pints at the Midland, we decided to check out the Over Sixties Club where The Ghosts were the resident Saturday night band. Bernie was on the door and he let us in for free. How's your dad? he asked me as he stamped our wrists. Bernie was The Ghosts manager, roadie and bouncer; his lad Trev played The Drums. The small bar was about six deep with blokes waiting to get served; it didn't help that the barman Arthur had a gammy hand. Down at the other end of the room, up on the little stage, The Ghosts had just launched into another Stones cover, *Tell Me*. Flo Lawrence was strutting his stuff; it could have been Mick Jagger. Fucking hell, this lot have got to be the ugliest band ever, Omo laughed. Yeah I know, and it's a fucking shame because they can play a bit. I knew them all from school; they were all the same age as me. Watching them play made me wish I could play the guitar and form a group. Omo nudged me in the ribs with his elbow. Have you seen who's here? he said, nodding his head across the room. I followed his gaze, and there she was over on the far side, sitting with her back to the wall, all alone. She looked sad and vulnerable, which seemed to add to her beauty. Well, what the fuck are you waiting for? Omo asked; he gave me a gentle push in the back. No, fuck it, it's bound to end in tears if I go over there, I told him, not sounding very convincing. See, I fucking told you. Look who's coming. I pointed him out: it was her boyfriend picking his way across the dance floor, drinks in his hand. Is that him? Omo laughed. What the fuck does she see in him? Come on, drink up, we're leaving, I told him, downing the rest of my pint. Fucking hell, we've only just got here, Omo complained. At least let's kick the shit out of him before we go. I looked at him in disbelief. Why do you think she's here with him instead of me? I already tried that, and that's why I'm stood here with you on a fucking Saturday night. Well, thanks a lot, Omo replied, trying to look hurt, a stupid grin breaking out across his face. All right, we'll have another one, and then we'll go; is that okay with you? Across the room her boyfriend got to his feet and made his way to the toilets. I waited until he had disappeared. Omo was still waiting to be served. Back in a minute, I told him, grabbing his arm.

The Ghosts were still going through their Stones repertoire. I'M GOING TO LOVE YOU NIGHT AND DAY, LOVE IS LOVE AND NOT FADE AWAY; really, The Ghosts ripping off the Stones ripping off Buddy Holly. Hello Jill, I said, as though I was greeting an old friend and not the love of my life. Jonty, what are you doing here? She smiled up at me, a warm smile that told me a million things and gave me a million reasons for this life. Do you fancy a dance? I asked her, holding out my hand. I'm with someone, she said after a slight hesitation; she turned her gaze to the floor. Yeah I know, I saw him. Come on, Jill, I'm not asking you to marry me, it's just one dance. She smiled and took my hand, and we walked onto the dance floor just as the song ended. Hold on, I said, leaning close to her ear. I made my way to the front of the stage. Flo, come here, I called, beckoning him over. All right, Jonty, what's up? he said, stepping down from the stage. Can you stop pretending to be the fucking Stones for a minute and play something else? Fuck off, he said grinning. What did you have in mind anyway? Some decent music; what about *You Better Believe It*, for Jill and me. Jill, he said, sounding surprised. I thought I saw her with someone else. You did, but hopefully not for much longer. They played it really well, SINCE I SAW THAT GIRL I CAN'T GET AWAY, NOW I GOTTA SEE HER EVERYDAY, YOU BETTER BELIEVE IT. Just for a few minutes I held her close, so close, you better believe it, and then it was over.

He was leaning back in his chair so that it balanced on two legs, trying hard to look nonchalant. Thanks for the dance, Jill, I winked at her. Yeah, now fuck off, he snarled, ruining his cool pose. I looked around the room exaggeratedly. Where are they, I don't see them. What the fuck are you on about? He was starting to lose it. I smiled at him. Your fucking friends, where are they? They must be here or you wouldn't tell me to fuck off; either that or you've got a short memory. He made no move to get out of his seat. I took a step towards him, and Jill stepped in front of me. Please, Jonty, don't start anything. *Me start anything? Fucking hell, Jill, here we go again,* I thought, stopping myself. It's all right, Jill, I'm going. Will you be all right, I said, putting my arm around her. Yes, she smiled; thanks, she added. Fucking pillhead! he shouted as I walked away, but I kept on walking.

It had been a good night, the best night in ages: out with my mates for a drink and a laugh, and seeing Jill had been the icing on the cake. I got up early Sunday morning. What Omo had said made sense; he was a good bloke, a real happy go lucky type. I wished I could be more like him. I really fancied a game. The works football team played on Sunday mornings so I decided to go along, hoping to get a game. My football bag was in its usual place in the cupboard under the stairs; when I unzipped it to put in a towel, my boots almost jumped out of the bag. There was white mould growing around the studs on top of a layer of caked-on mud. It took me a good half-hour to get them looking like football boots again. What's the matter with you? Mum said; are you feeling all right? Never felt better, I smiled at her. And a smile as well; your dad will never believe me. I set off for the ground, hoping I was going to be lucky; they had asked me often enough to play for them. Luckily, one of the lads was only too glad to drop out: he said he had a bad knee. I played under his name because I wasn't signed on: we won four one and I scored a hat trick. One or two of the lads hadn't wanted me to play. I was aware of this in the changing room. It turned out the lad who dropped out didn't have a bad knee; the manager left him out so I could play. It didn't make me feel very good either, but now all that was forgotten: I was the fucking hero. Fucking hell, I wish my dad had been there. Still, he would get to know at work, and I knew it would make him proud. Just for a short while I was on a high, without any help, and football became important again, but I knew it wouldn't last.

After the game, in the works social club everyone wanted to buy me a drink, even some of the opposition. I don't remember how many pints I had, but I felt fine until I left to walk home. Once I was out in the fresh air I just couldn't walk straight: it took me ten minutes to cross the road. Once I was on the other side, I clung to the wall and slowly headed for home. Through the terrible spinning haze that was my brain, I remember grinning stupidly at the strange looks I got from everyone who passed. When I eventually got home, I crawled upstairs and collapsed on the bed, just wanting to sleep. The moment I closed my eyes the room started to spin – it spun so fast, almost as though I had been sucked into the eye of a whirlpool. Staggering to my feet I straight away fell over, and when I was on my hands and knees I threw up. Sitting on the floor with my back to the bed, just for a short while I felt a bit better. Suddenly I had to piss; there was no way to make the bathroom on time so the window was the only option. Stumbling across the room I threw the window open and had the longest piss ever down over our back yard. Old Mrs Flint from next door let out a scream. I hadn't noticed her come out. There was nothing I could do to stop. Bert,

Bert! she screamed at the top of her voice. By the time Bert appeared I had stopped and shut the window. Getting back on the bed again I tried closing my eyes again, and this time it wasn't so bad. I lay listening to Mrs Flint telling Bert to do something. Cold beads of sweat soaked my hair and ran down my face and back. I was sick again, retching till there was nothing left. It was a good job the folks were out; fuck, I wouldn't want them seeing me like this. Drifting into sleep, vowing never to drink again, I dreamt of Jill and all the things we had talked about. We were married and had two children, a boy and a girl, but throughout the whole dream I was running after them, shouting for them to stop. Jill's hair was black, black as night; it made her even more beautiful.

Come on, son, it's time to get up, someone was shaking me, come on. I slowly opened my eyes. Dad was leaning over me. He turned and left the room when he saw I was awake, and the landing light spilled its brilliant glare across my eyes. When I raised my hand to shield my eyes I realised I was fully clothed and on top of the bed in a half sitting position. Memories of yesterday's drinking session were beginning to pound in my waking mind. I must have drifted off again because I felt him gently shake me again. This time he held a mug of tea in his hand. I reached out for it and took a sip: it was hot and sweet. They had a thing about sugar in our house. Mum and Dad both knew I didn't take it, but they always heaped about four spoonfuls in. Satisfied that this time I was awake, Dad left for work. I heard the front door close. I lay sipping the tea alone in the empty house, thinking about the dream

I'd had of Jill. It was the first time I had ever remembered a dream in its entirety and so clearly. Perhaps this meant something; perhaps dreams remembered became reality. Dragging myself out of bed, the hot sweet tea had lessened the pounding in my head. The vomit on the floor had gone; someone had cleaned it all up. The house smelt faintly of foundry dust, cast iron, hot sand and beeswax polish. It was a nice smell, familiar and somehow safe. Mum would be home soon from her night shift at the hospital. I poured her a cup of tea from the pot and ran to work without changing.

The days passed uneventfully. I never went out except to training on Tuesday and Thursday evenings. Jogging around the pitch on Thursday night, my heart skipped a beat when I saw two girls walking towards me, one of them with blonde hair. I thought it was Jill coming to see me, coming to ask me to go out with her again. Just for a few seconds I wanted to shout and tell the world, but it wasn't her. Going from deliriously happy to so sad in the blink of an eye made me realise just how much I loved her. I couldn't go on like this; I was going to have to do something.

Chapter Seven

Friday night, I was watching *Ready Steady Go*, when Roothy came staggering through our front gate. I could see he was pissed, so I jumped up and went outside before he could knock on the door. He sat down unsteadily on the little dividing wall between next door's and ours. Fucking hell, you look worse than I did, I said, sitting down beside him. He grinned at me from somewhere down by his knees. Let me guess. I bet there's a woman involved, I started to say. Suddenly, before I could stop him, he turned around and leaned over the wall and threw up on next door's front step. Mrs Flint's bright red door was flecked with sick running slowly down the paintwork. Fucking hell, not again. I jumped off the wall and pulled him to his feet. Come on, we'd better fucking go. He was laughing like a lunatic as I dragged him up the road and around the corner. He was sick again before we got much further; he looked awful, his hair stuck to his forehead and beads of sweat running down each side of his face. You look fucking terrible. Are you gonna be all right? I honestly thought he might keel over and fucking die. Light me a fucking fag, he said, sitting on the edge of the pavement. Fumbling in his pocket he handed me a crumpled pack of Park Drive. The smoke was bitter on the back of my throat; it had been a few months since I'd had a smoke. I feel a bit better, he said after a couple of drags; I don't think I'm going to be sick again. Sitting down next to him, I watched him blow smoke out the corner of his mouth, his hand shaking; he was a fucking mess.

Who is she, then? She must be something special to get you in this state. Who the fuck do you think it is? he said, spitting out a bit more bile. Not fucking Sue. I thought you were seeing someone else. That was fucking ages ago; I chucked her to get back with Sue. Fuck, not you as well; been there done that: what a fucking pair of losers.She says I'm trouble, he carried on without hearing me. Fucking hell, Jonty, I'm not that bad am I? Come on, you're my best mate, fucking tell me. She's not going to have you back if you're pissed all the time, I know that. He didn't say anything, just flicked the knub end of his fag into the road. Don't worry, she'll come round; you know what a stubborn fucker she is, I said, trying to sound cheerful. We started walking again, neither of us saying anything. Will you come with me to see her? he suddenly asked me. We could go round to her house now, she might listen to you. That's not a very good idea. Think about it. If we go round there now with you still half pissed, then you're gonna prove her right. He thought about it for a while. You're right, he said, but you will go with me tomorrow. Yeah, I'll go with you, but fucking hell, I can't even keep a girl of my own, I laughed. What the fuck went wrong with you and Jill, man? Roothy shook his head. I wish I knew, but people change, oh fuck it.

Saturday afternoon, I was on the bench for the first team. I would sooner have been playing for the reserves than sitting on my arse. It was a cup-tie, and there was quite a big crowd, around seven or eight hundred. The old man was standing at the back of the goal. I'd seen him when we were warming up. We had sort of acknowledged each other with a slight nod of the head, as though we were slight acquaintances. Shows of affection didn't come easy in our family. His drinking mates were with him, the ones he played dominoes with at the Railway. Just that slight eye contact that had passed between us told me how proud he was. Goughie the manager was in and out of the dugout like a fucking jack-in-the-box; he was making me nervous. Mind you, he had good reason; we were two nil down and fucking hopeless.Get warmed up, son, he said, leaning into the dugout and pulling me up. There was half an hour left when I trotted onto the pitch, the P/A system crackled into life and I heard my name announced. I got a huge cheer from behind the goal, which took away any nerves I had. We managed to pull a goal back, but it wasn't enough, and I didn't look out of place with the big boys.

When I was walking home after the game, I became aware of a couple of kids following me. I was halfway up our road when I stopped and turned around. They both stopped dead in their tracks. What did they want, the little fuckers? You play for the Town, don't you, one of them said, coming towards me. He held out a little green leather book and a pen: Can I have your autograph please? Me?

Are you sure it's me you want? I asked him, genuinely surprised that he should ask me. He nodded his head yes. I told you it was him, he said to his friend. I scribbled in his book with a signature that looked nothing like mine. I thought about crossing it out and doing it again, but he might have thought I was a right thick twat who didn't know his own name. I handed it back to him. Thanks Jonty, he beamed, showing his mate the book. I watched them run off happily down the road. *Wait till I tell Roothy about this,* I thought.

Sue stood at the front door with her arms tightly folded; this wasn't going to be easy. I told him yesterday that I didn't want anything to do with him anymore. Why, are you seeing someone else, then? I asked her. No I'm not, she snapped. Well, there you go, it won't do any harm to at least come out and talk to him. She said nothing, but she unfolded her arms. I don't think there's anything left to say, she eventually said, sounding close to tears. Look, Sue, I don't blame you if you don't want to see him, but honestly he is heartbroken. I don't know, Jonty; I don't think I can handle his drinking. It's just a word, Sue; I'm not asking you to fucking elope with him, for Christ's sake. She smiled for the first time. It's a bit awkward though. I've got my friend Moira here. I can't just leave her. Well, bring her with you. I'll keep her company while you two sort yourselves out. No, she won't do that, Sue shook her head; she don't like you. She don't like me? She don't even fucking know me, I said, feeling affronted. She says you're a wrong un. Oh, fuck it then, I said, turning to leave. Hold on, Sue grabbed my arm, I'll go and see if I can change her mind.

Roothy was sitting on the wall around the corner. That's it, then, she won't see me, he said, seeing me returning on my own. She's on her way, I smiled, joining him on the wall. He lit another fag. Fucking hell, what am I going to say to her? Roothy and Sue walked on ahead, and Moira stepped in with me. She gave me a nervous little smile, and I was surprised how good it felt to have a girl walking by my side again. Sue tells me you think I'm trouble, I said after a while. I never said that, she said, stopping and facing me. It's all right, I wouldn't blame you if you did, but not everything you hear is true, I said, winking at her. She had huge green eyes, which at that moment seemed to be sad, happy, hurt, but most of all kind. What, she said holding my gaze. Sorry, I was just lost for a moment, and I truly was. She frowned at me; I think Jill must be crazy, she blurted out. Her face turned red, and realising what she had said she turned away quickly. No, she did me a favour, I said, knowing it was a lie, at the same time convincing myself it wasn't. She smiled shyly at me, and looking into those huge eyes, I thought, *fuck it, here I go again.* Inside my head, a voice was telling me, stop this right now.

The Derwent Social Club was packed; the sound coming out of the open windows and doors was The Four Tops' *It's The Same old Song.* Saturday nights, Rastus was behind the turntables. He was a good bloke, apart from the fact he was a true Soul music freak. I went over to have a word with him, but mainly to see if he had anything decent to play. The only good thing I could find was *Please Stay* by The Cryin' Shames. I made him promise to play it later. I squeezed my way across the packed dance floor, into a blue fluorescent world under a flashing mirror ball moon. There must have been at least a hundred people in there, and the place wasn't much bigger than our front room. Well, look who's here, it's Tepper and fucking Bennett; how are you, lads? Harry said, towering over us. Harry ran the Derwent Social Club; he looked like a giant Captain Birdseye: no hair and a bushy grey beard. He had been in the navy during the war, and he reckoned he had been a bit of a hero; I believed him. He held out a huge hand. No hard feelings, boys. We both shook hands, his iron grip like a vice, and he looked us both in the eye: the message was as clear as day. Fucking hell, Harry, it was just a little misunderstanding, Roothy shouted to make himself heard.

Not so long ago, Roothy and me had been the Sunday night DJs at the Derwent, until we had fallen out with Harry, or rather Roothy had. Even now I still didn't know what it was all about; Harry and Roothy always had a kind of love hate relationship. Ain't there anywhere to sit, Harry? I asked him, standing on tiptoe to shout in his ear. Follow me, he said, leading us over to the far corner. Four young lads sat around a table looking like they'd lost a quid and found a tanner. They all wore dark off-the-peg suits and narrow black ties; all that was missing were the shades. Harry said something to them, and they got up and disappeared into the crowd on the dance floor. Who the fuck's that lot, Harry, the fucking Feds? Roothy laughed. Just my boys, Harry told him, smiling proudly. Yeah – fucking boys all right, Roothy said to the girls holding out a limp wrist behind Harry's back. For a moment the fallout between Roothy and Harry became a queer fantasy in my mind. I quickly dismissed it with a shiver as though someone was walking over my grave. Harry motioned us to sit down, gave a graceful bow to the girls and left. What was that all about? Moira wanted to know. Harry likes young boys, Roothy grinned; mind, he was in the navy.

How's it going? I asked him, as we stood at the bar waiting to be served. He shrugged his shoulders; I don't know, I'm just frightened of doing something wrong all the time. You know, sometimes I think is it fucking worth it? What if I can't change? Maybe I don't want to change, he added, almost in desperation. Anyway, what about you? he smiled. How do you mean? Come on, I can tell you fancy Moira. I don't fancy her; she's just a nice girl.Nice, yeah right; she's got a nice pair of tits, I know that. Well yeah, I had noticed that, I smiled. When we got back, two lads and two girls were sitting in our place. Moira and Sue stood nearby. What's going on? Roothy asked Sue. We only went to the ladies', she said, and they were sat there when we got back. Fucking idiots, Roothy nodded his head in the direction of Sue and Moira. They only went for a piss and left the fucking table. Fuck it, let's drink up and get out of here; it's too crowded anyway, I suggested. Fuck that, he said, and I could see trouble coming. Look, I thought you and Sue needed to talk, I reasoned. You can't hear yourself think in here, never mind talk. He shrugged his shoulders and downed his pint. I told the girls to drink up, we were leaving. Then it happened. Hey fuck face, we were sitting there, he said to one of the lads. That's right, pal, you were sitting there but not anymore. He looked a right mean ugly bastard; why the fuck did he always pick the hard fuckers? Oh fuck it, let's go, Roothy, said turning to me. He put his glass on the table with his left hand, and at the same time cracked the fucker at the side of the head with his right. For a second, it looked like he was going down, but he steadied himself and shook his head, felt his ear and started laughing. Suddenly he was on his feet, moving fast for a big man. He made a lunge at Roothy, and both of them went flying across the table, sending glasses and people scattering everywhere. They were rolling about on the floor, first one blue and then the other, under the flashing neon.

The big bloke's mate was looking around desperately, his eyes fixed on mine for a second, not knowing if he should be fighting me. In that brief look I could tell he didn't fancy it. I was glad. I just didn't want to fight anymore. Sue was screaming, and Moira looked close to tears. *That's fucked it,* I thought, *there's no way she's gonna have him back now.* He'll fucking kill him, the scared bloke said to me, and Rastus put on another shit Soul record. We waded in and pulled the big bloke to his feet. While we were still holding him, Roothy jumped up and smacked him in the mouth. Fucking hell, Roothy! I shouted as the big bloke shook himself free.

Luckily, Harry's boys appeared and pinned him down. Right, you two, out right now before I call the police, Harry said. It was him who started it, the big bloke protested, wiping his bloody mouth with the back of his hand. This is your last chance to leave quietly, Harry said, sounding very convincing. Come on, Tony, his mate said, picking up his jacket. Harry's boys let him go, and just for a moment you could see he was thinking about having another go; instead he started for the door. I'll have you, you little fuck, he said, turning at the door. Roothy blew him a kiss, which to me was like a death wish. Watching them leave I actually felt a little bit sorry for them. Roothy was a right cunt at times.

Sue and Moira had gone; considering the night they'd had it was no surprise. Well, that's fucked your chances up, I told him as he dabbed cold water on his split lip in the toilet mirror. Don't you mean your chances? he grinned at me through the mirror. Fuck off, I'm being serious here, knowing he was trying to get a rise out of me. That bastard's chipped me fucking tooth, he said, changing the subject. You're lucky that's all he did. Yeah, he was a big fucker, he laughed. What are you going to do about Sue? I asked him when we were back at the bar. Fuck her, the bitch, he said.

What a fucking shit night. That little dig about Moira that Roothy had made wasn't far from the truth; I liked her a lot. Still, something good did come out of it: Harry asked us if we would come back as his Sunday night DJs. I've really missed you two. Harry had his huge arms around us in a bear hug. This is a clean slate, lads. That little misunderstanding is water under the bridge, completely forgotten, he grinned. I was just about to ask him what the misunderstanding had been, when Roothy dug me in the ribs and shook his head no. Sunday nights just haven't been the same, Harry continued without seeming to notice. You mean your fucking takings are down, Roothy shot back. Harry gave him a hurt look. Come on, Harry, we were the best you've had; the place was packed every Sunday. For a minute I thought Roothy had blown it, but Harry's face broke into a grin. Same arrangement as last time, he said: a fiver each and all you can drink. Make it a tenner and you've got a deal. Roothy was pushing our luck. Harry stood up and ran his hand down the length of his beard. Let's call it seven, and I'll throw in some really good stuff; you are still pillheads, aren't you? He raised his hand in the air and clicked his fingers, and one of his boys appeared at his side with a little polythene bag. There's plenty more where that came from, he said, taking the bag and holding it up for us to see. Do you know how much these little pillheads pay for this? he said, handing the bag to Roothy. So we have a deal. He held out his hand. Okay, Harry, we said, shaking on it.

The advert in the local paper said, 'Sunday night, the return of Tepper and Bennett, seven o'clock till late at the Derwent Social Club.' Harry had also stuck flyers up all over town. I think maybe we should have changed our names, Roothy said, pulling a flyer off a lamppost. Tepper and Bennett was actually our little in-joke. [Tepper and Bennett], in brackets on the old green Columbia label, were the writers of some of The Shadows hits. The name just used to make us laugh, and The Shadows were fucking ace. We used to do that little Shads dance in the school playground. It sounds like a fucking circus act, he said, screwing up the flyer, and kicking it into someone's garden. Yeah, like a fucking pair of clowns, I joked. There was another flyer pinned to a tree a bit further down the road. How many has he put up, for fuck's sake? Roothy said. Read this one, I said, tapping the flyer. Someone had altered it to Topper and Ben. Now, that's much fucking better, Roothy laughed.

Chapter Eight

The place was packed, and Harry was a happy man. The only trouble was, we were playing music neither of us liked: all this fucking Soul shit. Being a Mod was my life really, but I just didn't buy it that they all liked fucking Soul music. Soulless music was more like it; maybe I should have been a Greabo. Still, the good outweighed the bad; it was cool getting paid to watch all the birds dancing and asking for requests. I had been hoping Jill might show, she would have known I was here, but I suppose her cunt of a boyfriend wouldn't be seen dead in a place like this.

I know her name, Roothy said, coming back with a couple of pints. What, whose name? I snapped at him, annoyed that he'd brought me another drink – more annoyed that Harry's deal of as much to drink as you like was turning him into an alcoholic. He didn't seem to notice my offhandedness. I know her name. That bird with the long hair, he continued; the one you've been eyeing up all night. I didn't deny it because he was right; he seemed to have a sixth sense when it came to my love life. What is it, then? I asked him. What's her name? Carol, he smiled, and you've got no fucking chance. She goes out with a ponce, he added. I looked at him blankly. She goes out with a fucking actor so he must be a ponce, right? I shrugged. How old do you think she is? He gave her a quick once-over. She must be about twenty-five, I reckon. Some little bird he had been chatting up all night was shouting to him to play some shit Supremes song, so I left him to it and went and stood at the bar next to her. It was getting late, and the place was thinning out quickly. I ordered a barley wine, even though I hated it, but it seemed different and cool. Sipping the barley wine, I couldn't think of anything witty or clever to say to her. Only stupid things floated into my brain; the best I could think of was: so your boyfriend's an actor? But that sounded pathetic; anyway, Roothy could have been making it up.

You've got lovely hair, she said to me. I turned to look at her. You should grow it longer, she smiled. That's what I was going to do anyway; Steve Marriott's started to grow his longer. Come here, she said. I moved closer, and she reached out and ran her fingers through my hair. Steve Marriott; so that tells me you don't like all this fucking shit you've been playing. Jesus, I didn't know any girls who swore. I'd never heard a girl say fuck, and for a moment it threw me. She was smiling sweetly at me, and I wanted her to say it again: it was wild and exciting. No, you're right, it is shit, but they like it, and the money's good. Then she said something strange. Tell me, Steve Marriott, what would you do for money? What would I do for money? I repeated. I was playing for time, trying to think of a clever answer. Would you let somebody fuck you? she said. I looked at her, knowing what I had heard her say but not quite believing it. Before I could answer, her sad face broke into a smile. I was just teasing you. I bet you think I'm some sort of weirdo, don't you? No, not at all, you seem quite normal compared to most of the people I know. She smiled at me. God, what sort of people do you go around with? she laughed. But I like you. I don't even know your name. It's John, but everyone calls me Jonty. And I'm Carol, she said, holding out her slender hand. Let's change the subject, Johnny; tell me what's your favourite record. *A Legal Matter* by The Who, I said without thinking, and then regretted it as loads of other great records came to mind. That's a great record, she agreed. Have you ever heard *I Fought The Law* by Bobby Fuller? she asked. How old are you anyway? she asked me, when I admitted I had never heard of Bobby Fuller. Twenty-one, I lied. She looked at me as though she was wondering what to do next. Have you got a car? she said eventually. Yeah, I said, the lies just tripping off my tongue, but I didn't come in it tonight. That's all right, I have mine, she smiled, finishing her drink. Fucking hell, she even had a car, I thought, frightened at any moment she was going to tell me to stop telling lies and fuck off and stop bothering her. Instead she said, Do you want to come back to mine and listen to Bobby Fuller? Yeah I'd love to, but what about your mum and dad? She burst out laughing and then apologised, I'm sorry, no, it's all right, I've got my own place. Why did I say that? *What a fucking twat*, I thought. Come on, then, she said, finishing her drink. By the way, he's dead, she added. I looked at her blankly. Who's dead? Bobby Fuller; the Mob killed him.

She drove a two-tone Triumph Herald convertible, with real leather seats and a walnut dashboard. Whatever she did for a living paid well. We drove into the city and parked in front of a block of high-rise apartments. The top floor, she said, pointing up as we stepped out of the car. In the light of the full moon I counted them: Twenty-five, I said aloud. There was a man sitting behind a desk reading a book inside the foyer. He stood up when he heard us enter. Good evening, Miss Copeland, he said, giving me the once-over. He was wearing a light grey uniform, with a red tie. Good morning, Horace, she corrected him. Horace glanced at his watch: It is indeed, he said. He kept staring at me as though he couldn't quite believe what he was seeing. I could feel his eyes watching me as we waited for the lift. She pressed twenty-five, and I gave Horace two fingers just as the doors closed. He needs to get out more, I said as I turned to see what I had done to upset Horace; mind you, that's some job reading a book and getting paid. The lift arrived at the top floor as though it had never left, and when we stepped out I expected to see Horace. My only experience of lifts was the ancient one in the Coop that took forever to go up just four floors, straining and creaking between each floor. I was trying to look nonchalant, but I knew she saw right through me. Acting like I knew it all. Fuck, if she hadn't have been there I wouldn't have known how to use the lift, I would have had to take the stairs.

We seemed to be halfway to the moon as we stood on the balcony, watching the twinkling lights going on forever, until they seemed to join the stars, like some huge black cape studded with thousands of sparkling sequins. She leant close to me, her long hair streaming out behind her in the cool night breeze. She pointed out all the interesting landmarks, her head resting on my shoulder; her hair smelt of lemons. Where do you live? she said, turning her face to mine. Show me. I looked to each horizon, and shook my head. Over the hill and far away: fuck, I was lost. She laughed. You're funny, she said, her lips so close I felt the words before I heard them. Well, I do my best, I said, in a voice that seemed strange and nothing like mine. Kiss me, Johnny. I wrapped my arms around her, the kiss was long and deep, tobacco and whiskey, and my Bazooka Joe. My head was spinning, and when I looked up into the night sky, I had a crazy feeling to jump off the balcony.

The next day I moved my things into her apartment, even bringing my cherished record collection. And so we lived in the clouds on the twenty-fifth floor, always on a permanent high one way or another. Looking back it was the beginning of the end.

Hey Jonty. Harry was motioning me over. He put his huge head down to my ear: Just be careful what you're getting into, he said. What the fuck are you on about, Harry? I gave him a puzzled look. He nodded towards Carol, who was sitting at the bar. It was exactly a week since that crazy night, and things couldn't have been any better. She turned around while we were both looking at her, and smiling she blew me a kiss. Fuck off, Harry, I said, pissed at him. Sorry, he said, but just be careful. Careful about what, Harry? Do you know something about her? I demanded, determined he wasn't going to spoil what we had. No, it's nothing like that, it's just, well, she's a lot older than you. So what? I laughed. Is that it, Harry? Are you worried about me? Come, on Jonty, do I have to spell it out? I mean, what's someone like her doing hanging around a place like this? I just get a bad feeling that's all. Harry, I'm a big boy now, I can look after myself, honest I can, dad, I smiled.

Life was at last feeling good again with Carol. We spent hours just lying on the floor listening to records, lost in the music, and high on whatever Carol brought home. She seemed to have an endless supply, introducing me to LSD. It was a crazy time, a time that cleared Jill out of my mind, a time I never went home, a time I packed in my football dreams. I never asked about her job; she told me she worked in an office, but it was some job. She left for work after me and was always home before me. She never mentioned her actor boyfriend, and I never asked, although the thought had crossed my mind that he was sending her money. Come on, we're going out, she announced one night. Out? I repeated, being sarcastic because we had got into the habit of never going anywhere. She took me to the pictures, and for the first time in weeks I thought about Jill and all the nights we had spent there; most of the time we never even knew what film was showing, we were so wrapped up in each other. The faint hum of the reels turning in the projection room was an old familiar sound, making me feel suddenly sad and missing my old life.

Which one is he? she said, jabbing me with her elbow. I looked at her in the flickering image of the screen. She wanted me to guess which one was her boyfriend. To be honest, I had begun to think he was a figment of her imagination. But her expression caught in the projection's harsh beam told me a different story. She turned to look at me, tiny specks of dust dancing between us. I was happy for her, but he was only an image. I looked at him up on the screen, not even flesh and blood, and he wasn't coming back. But I had a chance; she was real, and she loved me. My own happiness made me feel sorry for Carol. I put my arm around her shoulder and whispered in her ear. That's him, I just know, the bald-headed bloke with the big nose. She turned and looked at me, and seeing I was joking she stuffed a handful of popcorn in my mouth. The film was pretty awful, a plot full of holes, but he was a good-looking bloke, someone who was going to be a star. I bet he's shagging her, I said as we were walking home. Shagging who? she asked seriously. That dead fit bird he kept snogging in the film, I laughed, trying to make a joke out of it. You're right, he probably is, she said after a while. No, I was only joking, I told her. She gave me a half-hearted smile. Well, at least he's not a ponce, then, I said.

My plan to get Jill back had run into trouble: I didn't have a plan; I just couldn't think of any way to get her back. It didn't help that Carol had obviously picked up on my restlessness, and suddenly we were out almost every night to some party or another; it was amazing how many people she knew. Fucking weird parties they were too, not like the rich kids' parties we used to crash. These were kind of serious parties; fuck, there's no such thing as a serious party. What I mean is, these were grown-up parties, still plenty of drugs, even more drugs, but mainly people just sitting or standing around, and waiters coming round with food and drinks on little silver trays.

Hey you, man, stop fucking with the records, I heard someone say. I was doing my usual trick of going through the host's record collection. When I looked up to see who it was, a huge black fucker built like a brick shithouse was looking down at me. His face broke into a smile; find anything good? he said, sitting down next to me. Well, put it this way, there ain't anything worth nicking, I said. He laughed. Are you into music then, pretty boy? Yeah, I'm into music, but this ain't music, I said, dumping the pile of records in his lap. He looked at me wide-eyed for a moment, and then he started to laugh. Hey, you're a funny guy, pretty boy, I like you, he said, sifting through the records. You're right, these are all shit. He put them back under the record player. I suppose you're into all that Soul shit, I asked him. No, I can't stand it, he said; it's all you fucking little white boys who like that. Not this one, I laughed.

His name was Lenny, and he said he worked for the man. Are you with the party doll? he asked, pointing out Carol. If you mean Carol, then yes I am. Okay, then you work for the man too; he laughed and squeezed my shoulder with his huge hand. I hadn't a clue what he was on about. No, I don't work for the man, unless he owns the foundry, I said. Lenny looked at me with a quizzical look on his face, as though he didn't know if I was being serious or not. Who the fuck's the man anyway? I asked him. He started to laugh. Rizzo's the man, and he don't own no foundry, he said. Well, point him out, then, Lenny. He ain't here, man, he said; well, not yet anyhow. You know something, pretty boy, everybody at this party works for the man. Except for me, I reminded him. Yeah, except you, pretty boy, for now anyway, but if you're with the party doll, then you soon will one way or another. Carol don't work for the man, I persisted. She does, man, believe me, she really does. He looked at me for a long moment, as though he was deciding if he should continue or not. Finally he said, You really don't know, do you? No, what? I don't know what the fuck you're talking about. Carol works in an office, I know that much. I had this bad feeling where all this was leading, and I didn't want to know. Perhaps in the back of my mind I already did, but I couldn't come up with an answer. Aw, fuck it, Lenny said, getting to his feet. That's an expensive looking suit you're wearing, pretty boy; let me guess, the party doll bought it for you, he said. What if she did? I found myself defending her, even though I didn't give a fuck. How do you think she feeds her habit and yours: fucking uppers, downers, speed, LSD, acid? Did you know she's shooting up? he continued. Shut the fuck up! I shouted, jumping to my feet. My fists were clenched tightly, but I wasn't looking for a fight, in fact I was close to tears. Just ask her, pretty boy, Lenny said in a surprisingly gentle voice, just ask her, and get out while you can.

I sat alone for a very long time, trying to make sense of something I knew nothing about. A young girl came and sat down opposite me; she picked up the pile of records and started to look through them. There was something different about her, which I couldn't put my finger on, until it suddenly hit me, making me laugh out loud. She shot me a look that said don't you dare make fun of me. I'm sorry, I said, I wasn't laughing at you; it was just something I thought of. She smiled. It's okay, it's nice to find someone my own age. And that was it exactly; she took the words right out of my mouth. Find anything good in there? I said, pointing to the records. Not really, she said, it's all jazz stuff. Yeah, I know, I've already been through them, I smiled. There is this one though; she held up an album. "It's The Honeycombs." I pulled a face. I know, she said, that's what I thought, but wait till you hear this one track. She put it on the turntable, and fucking hell she was right. The track was called *Something I Got To Tell You*, and it was so fucking right. Something I got to tell you, baby, something giving me hell now, baby, when you're near me I'm strong, but when you're gone I'm all alone, I'm not alone for very long, I'm sorry, sorry I'm not worthy. We played that track over and over, until it was imprinted in our minds forever. When we left the party, I realised I didn't even know the girl's name or what she had been doing there. I thought about her constantly over the coming months, until I convinced myself she wasn't real.

That night after the party as we lay in bed, she said, He told you, didn't he? I didn't answer. Lenny told you, she persisted; I saw you talking to him. He didn't tell me anything, I said at last. Liar, she said. Look, Carol, he didn't tell me anything that I didn't already know: that you're a junkie, and I'm going the same way. He told you what I do, didn't he? She didn't seem to mind being called a junkie. They're all rich and respectable, and I only fuck the ones I want to. At last it all came together: where the money came from, how she could afford this penthouse apartment. She was a fucking whore, and I was a stupid fucking idiot. I should have just walked out there and then, but I listened while she told me everything.

Well, fucking say something! she screamed at me, when I remained silent. Dawn was already peeping through the windows, and in the half-light I could make out her tear-stained face. What do you want me to say, Carol: that everything's all right, that I don't mind? I suddenly felt exhausted, weak and tired, the realisation that I was lost like a ship without a rudder had come in the window like a huge wake-up call on the first rays of daylight. Nothing's changed really, I heard her say; we've got it good haven't we? All the money we need, and this apartment. Is this where you bring them? I asked her. She said nothing. I looked at her; she was more lost than me. It doesn't mean anything, she said, sounding desperate; it's just you, you know that, don't you? I hated her desperation. I hated her. I hated myself. So this Rizzo bloke, he's your pimp, he supplies your clients, you work for the man, I said, answering my own questions. How much do you get to keep, how much of the money does he let you keep? Fifty fifty, she said, sounding a little less desperate, perhaps surprised I was still there. Rizzo, he's not that smart, he thinks he's getting half, but it's more like seventy thirty, she smiled. She reached out and ran her fingers through my hair.

Tell me what you do, I heard myself say. She raised herself up on one elbow. What? she said. With these men that come around, what do you do to them, what do they do to you? I want to know. She lay her head back down on the pillow and let out a sigh. Do you suck their cocks? Do they cum in your mouth? There was no reply. Please, Carol, tell me, I need to know, please, Carol, you owe me this much at least. Don't make me do this, Johnny, it's not what you want, it won't do any good, but her voice had a resignation to it, and I didn't care anymore. She told me all the things she did, and I felt myself slowly becoming aroused. Turned on by the thought of her being fucked by all these different nameless men. Reaching for her hand I put it around my hard cock. I fucked her, while she whispered in my ear that mine was the biggest cock she had ever had, while tears rolled down her face.

Every night became the same: she would tell me what she had done during the day, while we fucked. She no longer hid the marks on her arm from shooting up, although she never did it in front of me. I kept thinking back to the party, to the girl and the song and the realisation that I wanted my old life back. But I was still here. I looked at Carol; she looked like death warmed up. Someone had to help her. You'll end up dead taking that shit, I said. Promise me that you won't leave, and I swear I will never take heroin again, she said. Her skin was grey and blotchy; her once shiny long hair hung stringy and matted around her face. Carol, I'm still here, aren't I? That's not an answer, she said. I looked in the bathroom mirror to check my reflection; Carol's appearance had got me worried about my own looks. The face that stared back told me to get out before it was too late. Swear to me that you'll quit drugs, Carol, not just heroin, and I'll stay and help you. She seemed so pleased, so happy, and for a brief moment the happiness brought her back. But I knew it was only a flicker of false hope – she was lost – and I was gone as soon as possible.

Chapter Nine

Jonty, I heard someone calling from across the street. Sue was waving at me, waiting for the traffic to pass. Moira was with her, so I checked my reflection in a shop window. I hadn't seen either of them since that night at the Derwent, and I'd never had the chance to apologise to Moira. I watched them run across the road. Jill's pregnant, Sue blurted out breathlessly. I was thinking about the first time I had seen Moira, when Sue had told me that Jill had broken up with her boyfriend. This was almost déjà vu. I had heard what she had said, but it didn't register. I said nothing but I could feel them both waiting for my reaction. So what? I managed at last, belatedly trying to pull myself together. I saw disappointment in Moira's eyes, before she averted her gaze down to her feet. Sue took my arm and led me away. I don't think you understand, she said. I looked at her blankly. Jill told me she's not sure who the father is. *Fucking whore,* I thought, and then I realised what she was saying. How far gone is she? I asked her. About three months; you should go and see her, Sue added. It's mine, I said to myself. Go and see her, Sue said, walking away. Moira looked back and smiled at me, a sad smile.

At half past six that night I was standing across the road from Jill's house. She lived in a detached house, where everyone had neat front lawns with little flowerbeds around the edge and paved driveways; it was a nice area. It was a cold damp late October day, the clocks had just changed, hurrying on the night, and for once I was glad of the dark. A fine rain was falling steadily; it was so fine that I could not even see it in the glare of the street lamps. My thin cotton windbreaker was wet through under my fingers as I turned my collar up in a hopeful gesture. I walked down the side of the house, still seeking the darkness, and remembering that hot summer night three months ago in this very spot. Jill's mum opened the door, and the light from the house spilled out all over me. I put my hand up to shield my eyes. Oh, I heard her say. She sounded disappointed, and she looked as though she had been expecting someone else. Hello Mrs Brown, I'm sorry to bother you, but I was wondering, is Jill in? I said. She said nothing, and I knew she was thinking of some excuse to get rid of me. It won't take a minute, I just need to return something to her, I lied. She stuck her head out of the door, and looked down the driveway. Yes, dear, yes, she's upstairs getting ready to go out, she said, gathering herself together and giving me a forced smile that must have almost killed her. Come on in, John, she said, still smiling; get out of the rain. I stepped inside, and wiped my feet on the doormat. I'll just go and get her, she said, walking along the hallway to the bottom of the stairs. Thank you, Mrs Brown, I called after her.

I remembered the last time I had been here; the bitch had looked down her nose at me. Almost as though I had been casing the joint, to come back later and steal her fucking silver. Why was she being so nice? Then it dawned on me. She was taking the piss, safe in the knowledge her precious daughter was going steady with someone who met with her approval. It was obvious she had no idea that her daughter was up the fucking duff. I smiled to myself. I could hear a muffled conversation from somewhere at the top of the stairs. She came back down a few moments later and showed me into the front room. Jill won't be a minute, dear, she smiled.

The room was cold; it was only used for special occasions like Christmas. Somehow I don't think I was a special occasion, or maybe she thought I was. I looked around the room, which Jill had said was her mother's pride and joy. A writing desk stood along one wall, a walnut china cabinet along another. On top of the writing desk a silver tray held several bottles: whiskey, sherry, port. The china cabinet was full of Mr Brown's collection of cigarette lighters, carefully arranged according to size over two of the three shelves. It didn't make sense to me; if we had a best room in our house we would use it. For all its eloquence it was somehow a sad neglected room, where even if they lit the fire it would still be cold. I shivered inside my wet jacket and thought about sitting down in my damp clothes on the imitation leather settee.

Lost in my thoughts, I didn't hear her come in. She was standing with her back to the door, as though she was keeping someone out. He will be here soon, she said, looking past me and out of the window. Well it's nice to see you too, I said sarcastically, immediately wishing I hadn't. Perhaps that was our problem; we seemed to bring out the best in each other but also the worst. I'm sorry, Jill, I haven't come here to cause an argument. Well, that will be a first, she muttered, moving away from the door. Jesus fucking Christ, the life I was living was all because of this girl standing before me. The love I felt for her, the love I had hidden in denial, was laid bare for her to see. Fuck, why hadn't I done something about this before? Why wasn't I doing something now? I walked towards the window, but she stepped in front of me. Just for a moment I thought she wanted me to wrap her in my arms, but instead she said, Please can you sit down or someone might see you. I shook my head but sat down. The curtains won't close, she said; they don't meet in the middle, and so we never close them. The best room in the house and the curtains didn't fit. I wanted to laugh. Oh, was all I managed.

She sat down next to me. I suppose you've been talking to Sue, she said. It occurred to me at that moment that she had obviously wanted me to know; she knew that Sue would tell me. Somehow this gave me a glimmer of hope. Does your mum know? I asked her. She looked at me, the way she had always looked at me, and in her eyes I saw the love she had for me, the love she would always have. No, she said eventually, still looking into my eyes. I was waiting for the right moment, she managed a smile. We could tell her now, I said. You seem certain it's yours, she said.I watched her playing nervously with her handkerchief, which she was wrapping and unwrapping around her fingers. Tell me it's not mine, I asked her. He thinks it's his, she said after a long silence. Fucking hell, Jill, you've told him. I don't believe you. Why, for fuck's sake? He wants to marry me, she said as if that made it all right. But it's not his baby, and you know it, I said calmly. It might be, she said, tears welling up in her eyes. Reaching out my hand, I put my fingers under her chin and turned her face towards mine. One little tear escaped from her eye and ran slowly down her face. I wiped it away with my finger. Don't tell me you forgot that night three months ago, I said.

Her shoulders began to shake as she fought back her tears. I couldn't stand to see her crying. Look at me, Jill; do you love him? I asked her. She didn't answer, and the tears dropped into her lap. It's simple, Jill: you do or you don't, I persisted. I don't know, she sobbed. You don't know? Fucking hell, Jill ,that's not an answer. Do you love me? I asked her. You know I do, she said. That was all I wanted to hear, and at that moment I felt like I had never felt before. She loved me; I had a lump in my throat and a million thoughts of where that love would take us. But it's not that simple, I heard her say. I could feel myself deflating like a burst balloon. You just told me that you love me. I do, but it's not enough, she said. I got up and started to pace the room. Please sit down. Don't go near the window, she pleaded, pulling at my arm. Fuck the window! I shouted. See, that's what I mean; you're trouble, Jonty, everyone says so, you're just not reliable, you're a mess, and I just can't cope with that. I'm a mess? Just take a look at yourself, I shot back. Sorry, I said, sitting back down and taking hold of her hands. I can change, I can honestly. In fact, I want to change, I need to, believe me. I want to settle down. I sounded desperate, which I was, and I didn't care.

Her tears had stopped, and she was looking at me intensely. Right at that moment I felt as though I could have reached into her very soul and pulled out what she wanted to say. But in the blink of an eye it was gone, and I simply waited for the answer I knew was coming. You better go, she said tenderly. Not until you answer me. She slowly shook her head. It wouldn't work. You just told me you love me, I interrupted her. Jill, we love each other, and you know what they say: love conquers all. He's got a good job; they're going to make him a manager. That was her mother talking, the fucking bitch. Let's get married, Jill; just come away with me now. I put my arms around her and felt her familiar closeness, regretting all the time I had wasted with Carol. I felt her arms holding me, her lips kissing my neck. I don't care even if the baby isn't mine, it doesn't matter; we belong together, I said, kissing her eyes, her mouth, her nose. Stop it, she begged, starting to cry again. She pushed me away. You say you love me, so prove it and go, please, Jonty, I mean it, she pleaded.

We sat in silence for what seemed like forever, a sad resigned finality hanging over us. My head was pounding, my ears ringing with thoughts I would never say. Getting to my feet, I heard myself say in a faraway strange voice: When I walk out of that door, Jill, that's it, I won't be coming back; you can't change your mind. She said nothing, her head down, sobbing for whom I did not know. My legs suddenly felt as though they were made out of lead, and I sort of half ran half stumbled out of the house, like a drunk looking for the door. Bye, dear, I heard her mother say, and for once sarcasm was lost.

Outside, I started to cry, taking in huge gulps of air to try and get myself together. Next door, a man walking his dog stopped to unlock his front door, key poised in his hand. What the fuck are you looking at? I said to him. He quickly went inside. I crossed the road and leaned against the wall and waited. I remembered something my dad had once said: If you're going to cry, make sure it's something worth crying about. *What fucking bollocks was that,* I thought.

She was right: I didn't have to wait long. Within a couple of minutes a big saloon car pulled up outside her house. Flash bastard, I watched him turn on the interior light and comb his hair in the rear-view mirror. Inside the house the light had gone out in the front room where I had been standing just a few minutes before. Satisfied with his hair, he got out of the car and stood a moment admiring it. Bending down, he rubbed at some imaginary mark on the wing, before striding confidently through the front gate. I knew it wouldn't last: everything about him was wrong. I wanted to run across the road and tell him all the little things I knew about her, things he would probably never know. How she couldn't stand to have her knees touched, about the tiny scar on the palm of her hand that looked just like another lifeline. The pattern of freckles on the inside of her thigh that was exactly the same as the stars that made up the Plough. I could have told him a hundred things about her, as she could have of me. Instead I walked away. Pausing to look back, I saw the light go on again in that lonely cold room. Silhouettes spilled onto the front lawn. I walked back to his car and kicked a big dent where his imaginary mark had been, with the heel of my boot. Fuck it, I said to myself, but I still didn't feel any better.

Chapter Ten

Carol had become not only dependent on heroin, but she was dependent on me, her hollow promises born out of my own unsympathetic attitude. She had become a lost cause; the drugs were ruining her once good looks, and slowly her life. The only good thing to come out of my time with Carol was my complete aversion to drugs of any kind; now I wouldn't even swallow an aspirin. For a week after I had been to see Jill, I hung around the flat, hoping she would change her mind. But I was fighting the forces of her mother, and hope was all I had. You're going to leave me, aren't you? she accused me one day. You're going to go back to that little schoolgirl. Even in her spaced-out mind she knew I just didn't care. I had even taken to blaming her as much as Jill's mother for us not being together. And then the tears would start. Please don't leave me; I can't live without you, she would sob. Carol, you need help, professional help; I can't give you that. Please, I can stop, I don't need this fucking shit, she said, throwing a plastic bag with all her gear onto the floor at my feet. Get rid of it. Throw it off the balcony! she shouted. I picked it up.

But it wouldn't have made any difference; I knew she had plenty more. Can you stop working for Rizzo? Can you stop working for the man? I asked her. Absolutely, yes, she said. Okay good, that's a start. You need to tell him, Carol, because at the moment he fucking owns you. Get away from him, and maybe we can start to get our lives together. I swear for nearly a week she did try, and for that I really admired her. The thought that she must really love me came as a shock. I always thought of the actor as the love of her life; I was just a substitute until he returned. Her love was unrequited, as it always had been. But if I could somehow help to get her away from Rizzo, then maybe I could leave without too much hurt.

It was just a week before Christmas, a Wednesday afternoon; I was waiting for the lift in the lobby. Horace was giving me the evil eye as usual; for some reason he didn't like me. Maybe he was jealous because he fancied Carol, but I had a feeling it was more than that. The lift arrived, and when the doors opened two men stepped out. I could see them looking back at me as the doors closed; they were laughing at something. I had never seen them before, but I was certain they worked for the man: they were Rizzo's men. She was sitting on the sofa, her head down, her long black hair covering her face. The bad feeling I had coming up in the lift subsided a little. Are you okay? I said, moving closer. What did those two want? I stopped dead as she looked up: her left eye was swollen, her nose and mouth bleeding. Drops of blood landed silently on the floor at her feet. She tried to speak but instead cried out in pain. She really should have gone to hospital, but she shook her head no. Let me call a doctor, then. I'm all right, she mumbled, holding her hand up to her bleeding mouth. After I had cleaned and washed her face, she seemed a little brighter. How do I look? she asked. Not too bad after all, I told her. Liar, she smiled. Ouch, she grimaced, touching her swollen mouth. Her bottom lip probably needed a couple of stitches. Let me send for the doctor, I tried again. I'm okay, really I am, she said, taking my hand. Is this because you told him you don't work for him anymore? No, she said, I didn't tell him. I was waiting for the right time. Then why? I asked her. I don't know. All they said was that Rizzo said I had to work harder: he wants more money. How the hell are you going to do that looking like— I stopped short, realising what I was saying. Pass me my mirror, she said, pointing to her handbag. I've told you how you look; just get some rest, Carol. You'll look much better in the morning. Lie down with me, then, she said, moving over to make room.

Falling into a deep sleep, I eventually awoke to find her gone. It was still dark outside, and the only light crept under the bathroom door. She was standing in front of the mirror, her makeup bag close at hand. This isn't going to work, she said calmly to my reflection looking over her shoulder. How the hell am I going to work looking like this? Who's going to want me now? Tears had started to well up in her eyes and now they ran freely down her face, smearing her makeup and giving her the appearance of some kind of grotesque clown. It's okay; honest, in a couple of days, a week at most, you'll look as good as new. Promise, she said. Promise, but you can say goodbye to this place; we've got to get out. I didn't know where we were going to go, but I had to think of something, for my sake as well as hers. I had to get my life back; I had to get Jill back.

Three days after Carol's beating, a big black Zephyr pulled up alongside me as I walked home from work. At first I thought it was the cops, until the door opened and this skinny youth dressed in a really sharp suit got out. I walked on, minding my own business, but the skinny youth caught up with me. Then I recognised him as one of the blokes who had stepped out of the lift the other night: one of the blokes who had worked Carol over. I glanced past him to look at the driver; it was a black guy who I didn't recognise. The thought crossed my mind to leg it. I knew I could easily outrun this one. We stood eyeing each other up, and I could tell he knew what I was thinking: a slight smile played around the corners of his mouth. I looked over at the car again; the radio was playing some Soul shit, and he was drumming his fingers along the top of the steering wheel, keeping time with the song. The man wants to see you, the skinny youth said, interrupting my thoughts of escape. What the fuck are you talking about? I said. His face went blank for a moment, as though I had given the wrong answer. Then he turned to the driver, who shrugged his shoulders and cupped his hand to his ear, Mr Rizzo wants to see you, he tried again. Well, why didn't you say so in the first place? I smiled at him. He turned again to look at the driver, who mouthed the words, fucking hurry up. Black cunt, he said, turning back to face me. Tell Mr Rizzo if he wants to see me, then

I'm sure he knows where to find me, I said, starting to walk away. The skinny youth stepped in front of me, and behind me the driver got out and held open the back door of the car. Stop trying to be a clever fucker and get in the fucking car, he said menacingly. The black guy looked a right mean hard bastard close up, unlike the skinny one. Across the road and coming this way I could see Omo, Joe and a couple of other lads. Hey Omo, you fat fuck, come over here, I shouted. Rizzo's boys exchanged glances, as the four of them came over. You all right, Jonty? Omo said. I don't know, am I all right, fellas? I said, looking at them. Come on, Billy, let's go, the black guy said, getting back in the car. Billy stood his ground and looked at all of us in turn, a lopsided grin on his face. What the fuck's your problem? Omo said, towering over him. He likes hitting women, don't you, Billy? That's his problem, I said. Billy looked like he might explode at any moment. Get in the fucking car! the black guy shouted. Billy got in slowly and wound the window down. I'll have you, you fucking ponces, he sneered, leaning out of the window. For a big bloke Omo moved surprisingly fast; before the car could pull away his fist slammed through the open window, into Billy's surprised face. The car sped away, Billy holding his nose and still shouting the odds. Who the fuck was that? Omo asked, as they disappeared into the traffic. You don't want to know, Omo, believe me; thanks anyway, I said. Declining an offer to go to the Duke with them. They were good mates, and a night on the piss was very tempting. I watched them go, all free and single, not a fucking care in the world. Hey, I owe you one, I shouted after them.

Carol was sitting on the sofa watching the telly, her long legs tucked under her. She had washed her hair, and her makeup was at last hiding the bruises. The swelling around her eye and mouth had almost gone, and at a glance she looked like the pretty girl I had first met. See, I told you, I said, sitting next to her, as good as new. I gently ran my finger across her cheek under her eye; close up, she smelt fresh and new. Does it hurt? I asked her. She shook her head smiling. Rizzo's been on the phone, she said, lifting her eyes to look at me. Oh yeah, and what did he want? He said I had to get back to work and pay him the money I owe him. She looked away, and neither of us spoke. I hope you told him to go fuck himself, I said at last, knowing it was a stupid thing to say. I thought about telling her about my little run-in with Rizzo's goons, but that would only worry her more. I'm sorry, I shouldn't have said that, but, Carol, you can't go on like this. Don't you think I know that? she shouted. But what can I do? I don't have the money to pay him back. I couldn't believe what she was saying. Pay him back? Carol, you don't owe him anything; if you did he took what was owed out of your face. Fucking hell, Carol, he sent two thugs round here to work you over, and he wants paying back. We sat in silence once more. Maybe she was right: there was no way out, Rizzo was her pimp, and he really did own her. Jesus fucking Christ, I had to get out of this mess, it was nothing to do with me. Obviously, though, it was, or why else did he want to see me? And for the first time I began to feel a little bit scared. You're going to go, I heard her say, breaking the silence; it's written all over your face. I started to say something, but she stopped me. It's all right, honestly, no tears this time I promise, she said, taking my hand in hers. I want you to go, Johnny; this is my problem not yours. Carol, there must be somewhere you can go; just get in the car and drive away. The car's gone, she said calmly; they took it when they paid their little visit. She seemed oddly serene and beautiful in her resignation, as though she had explored every escape route and found none. What if I could find us somewhere, I heard myself say. She squeezed my hand and tears welled up in her eyes. No, she said, it's too late.

Horace never even asked any questions; if he knew what Carol had been doing for a living, he didn't let on. Once he knew that she needed help, and that I was trying to help her, his suspicion of me disappeared. She could stay at his place for as long as she liked; he was so much in love with her, he couldn't believe his luck. We left the next morning, at the end of Horace's shift, all Carol's belongings in the back of his car.

I set off for work feeling better than I had done for a long time, some sort of plan forming in my mind. I was halfway out of the Carol thing, she had said as much herself; now all I needed to do was win back Jill. I was going to get myself fit again and give football another go. Fucking hell, not again. The big black Zephyr came from nowhere, screeching to a halt, shattering my thoughts. Billy jumped out; he had a plaster across the bridge of his nose, which was swollen a bluish purple colour and caked in dried blood. Get in the fucking car, cunt. He jabbed something in my ribs to help me along. I looked down and saw it was a gun; my first thought was that he had to be kidding, and it wasn't a real gun. I took another look, and decided it was. Jesus, what the fuck was I involved in?

He opened the back door and shoved me in, and then sat down beside me. The black guy was behind the wheel again. Okay? he said, over his shoulder to Billy. Yeah, not a fucking peep, Billy laughed. The car moved off into the morning traffic. I was going to be late for work, I thought. What's the matter, smart arse, cat got your tongue? Billy grinned. What a fucking idiot, I was so naïve; I should have seen this coming a mile away. The feel of Billy's gun sticking in my ribs had made me realise too late just who we were dealing with. The thought that they probably already knew Carol had gone made me sick to my stomach. Was this why they had picked me up? Hey, where are we going? I said to the driver, ignoring Billy.Like I told you the other day, he said, the man wants to see you. Next to me, Billy started to laugh. Yeah, the man wants to see you, and after that you're all mine. I don't know why, but I just couldn't stop myself. Fucking hell, Billy, you're a real hard man with that in your hand, I heard myself say. For a moment Billy's face registered total confusion, and then his cheeks started to colour. That nose of yours looks sore. I reckon it's broken, I said, starting to enjoy myself. Leave it, Billy, the black guy said, he's just trying to rile you. Billy's eyes had taken on a wild unfocused edge, as though at any minute he might explode. Fuck it, in for a penny; I was in all right. You should get that nose seen to, because if it mends like that you're gonna be even more ugly than you are now. Billy backhanded me across the mouth. Fucking hell, Billy, are you fucking mad? the black guy shouted. What the fuck's Rizzo gonna say? I ran my tongue over my split lip, exploring the cut with the tip; the blood tasted like liquid metal. The black guy was looking at me in the rear-view mirror; he shook his head when I caught his eye. You can explain this to Rizzo, he said to Billy. He fucking asked for it, Billy complained. Just shut the fuck up, Billy, – the black guy sounded well pissed – and put that fucking gun away before you shoot somebody. Billy sat back in the corner, sulking and playing with his gun; he aimed it at the back of the driver's head and pretended to pull the trigger.

After about twenty minutes we pulled into a potholed car park at the back of a two-storey red brick building. The car stopped at the side of a rusty fire escape; Billy got out and pointed the gun at me. Put that fucking thing away, the black guy said when he saw the gun. He threw his hands up in a helpless gesture. You can't get the staff these days, he said to me as I got out of the car. He motioned for me to go up the fire escape, and he followed close behind. The steps rang out hollow underfoot, and tiny pieces of grey paint dropped to the ground under our weight. At the top he leaned over me and rang the bell at the side of the door; it sounded so loud that I half expected the fire brigade or the cops to suddenly turn up. I looked around hopefully but none appeared. On the other side of the door, the sound of bolts being pulled and chains unlatched could be heard. Behind me, Billy had joined us; he grinned at me menacingly, which he seemed to do a lot. Someone silently opened the door, while Billy had my attention.We all stepped inside, but whoever had opened the door was nowhere to be seen. A dimly lit corridor appeared in front of us; we started walking down it, discovering several other doors on either side as my eyes became accustomed to the gloom. The corridor ended with another door, this time facing us. The black guy knocked once and went inside. I glanced at Billy leaning against the wall under one of the bare red light bulbs. Behind him, down the corridor, two more could be seen, giving the place the feel of some ghostly ship. Billy was playing with his pocket watch, which hung from a gold chain attached to the waistcoat of his expensive looking three-piece suit. He might have been a prick but he was a prick with style. What the fuck are you grinning at? he sneered, which seemed to be his only other expression. I smiled at him, and winced as my split lip cracked open again and a trickle of blood ran slowly down my chin. I wiped it off with the back of my hand and noticed my own clothes. I had on my work gear: a boiler suit, which I'd got my mum to taper, big steel-toe-capped boots with the metal showing through the leather, and an old US army jacket with the epaulettes hanging loose. My snap bag was still on my shoulder, with sandwiches and a hot flask of coffee inside. *And they say crime doesn't pay*, I thought. The door opened again, with the black guy standing half in and half out; he silently ushered me inside then went out and closed the door behind him.

An overpowering smell of cheap cologne filled the air inside the room, a pungent sickly midnight on the bog scent that pervaded my nostrils and the back of my throat. Come on in and sit down, a voice sounded from the other side of the room. I looked towards it, towards the only light in the room. It was no more than a 15-watt bulb that flickered dimly in the distance. I slowly made my way towards it, careful not to walk into anything. The dim light was spreading its meagre brightness across a desk, behind which I could make out a figure. He looked small behind the desk or maybe the desk was big. As I got closer, the thought that maybe he was an albino crossed my mind; I had read something once about albinos and light. And then I saw him: he was no albino, just another fucking nigger. I should have known with a name like Rizzo.

It's Johnny, am I right? he said, swinging his legs up and resting his fancy suede Chelsea boots on the top of the desk. Take a seat; he motioned to a chrome leather chair opposite him. His voice sounded like a little kid's, as though it hadn't broken yet. Comfy, don't you think? he smiled down at me, flashing a couple of gold teeth. I felt as though I was sitting on the floor, the chair was so low, giving him an advantage. Johnny, he started to say, you don't mind if I call you Johnny, do you? No, I don't mind. Good, he smiled. I hear you led my boys a merry little dance the other day. He paused and waited for me to say something. I can tell you've got a certain something, he continued at my silence. You seem to possess a bit of the old grey matter, something I admire. He spoke in a really posh voice; he was someone from money and well educated. The posh accent and the high voice made him sound like a queer. Yes, that was it: he was a fucking queer. Queer spotting was something I had inherited from my dad; he could spot a queer a mile away. I must apologise for the injury you sustained, he said, touching his bottom lip. Rest assured, young Billy will be admonished. Young Billy, I laughed. What are you, the fucking headmaster? Well yes, I suppose you could put it like that; in fact, that is a very apt way of putting it.

He was a fucking raving queer, that was certain; I began to worry what he wanted with me. He must have seen the look I gave him. We are not all from the jungle, you know; perhaps I disappoint you. I don't know what you're talking about, all I know is you're costing me money; I should be at work. He started to laugh. Ah yes money, well, that's why you are here, to discuss money, my money. Johnny, he sighed. Johnny, he said again, as though he hadn't got it right the first time. I hate talking about debts; I find it somewhat embarrassing. He leaned back with his hands behind his head. I didn't believe a word of it: he was enjoying every minute. Putting it simply, he was saying, you have been living at my expense. He paused and crossed one foot over the other. Now, as I'm sure you know, Carol was pulling a little con trick on me, but I think we've sorted that out, he laughed. He waited for my reaction, but I stayed silent. You know, you just might have put her up to it, but none of that matters now; that's all irrelevant. He waved his hand, dismissing that particular thought. Now, what is important is for you to cancel your debt, settle your account in the form of a little favour. Just a minute, I interrupted him, I don't owe you anything. Well, Johnny, I beg to differ; for a start, you have been living rent-free at my apartment, am I right? What could I say? That I thought it was Carol's apartment? Which I did, at least at first; no one could be that naïve. Don't tell me you earn enough to pay for the lifestyle you have been living. He carried on without waiting for me to answer. What you earn in a week wouldn't keep me in cigars for a day. My money has been buying you all your fancy clothes, all your drugs, and let's not forget your love of music: all those records you've been buying. He seemed to know quite a lot about me. I hear you have quite a collection, he continued. You seem to hear a lot of things, I began, but he cut me off mid-sentence. Please let me finish, he said, holding up his hand. In a perverse kind of way I admire you; you're prepared to sleep with a woman, knowing that she sleeps with other men for money. He shook his head slowly. Not a lot of men would do that, but the fact remains that you have been living off immoral earnings. He started to laugh as though he had just thought of it. So you see, it doesn't really matter if it's mine or if it's Carol's: there's no difference, do you understand what I'm saying? he smiled. Oh yeah, I understood all right. The bastard thought he had me, and just for a moment he did. I nodded my head that I understood. Good, he smiled, I could tell you were smarter. Now then, the little favour I need you to do for me.

Everybody works for the man, am I right? I mimicked him. He looked at me and gave a little laugh, but ignored the remark. Your friend Harry, he began, the one who owns the Derwent Club… let's see how can I put this. He paused and took a cigar from the top pocket of his jacket, ran it under his nose and then put it back in his pocket. The smell of a good cigar; it almost seems a shame to set fire to them, he said more to himself. Your friend

Harry, seems to be treading on my toes, taking one or two of my customers. His way of getting to the point of a subject was almost laughable, but I could see where he was heading. Maybe you can have a word with him on my behalf, convince him. Convince him of what exactly? I interrupted him. Why don't you just send a few heavies round and bang some heads together; that should do the trick. Rizzo started to laugh; Johnny, Johnny, I have my reputation to think of, friends in high places, you know, he added mysteriously. I didn't know nor did I want to: none of this was anything to do with me. Rizzo had taken his feet off the table and replaced them with his elbows; he looked at me intently, waiting for an answer. So what you're saying is you want Harry to stop dealing, I asked him. No, no, I don't mind him selling stuff, I just want him selling my stuff, he said, pushing back his chair and getting to his feet. Suppose he won't agree? Harry's his own man, he doesn't take shit from anyone. Even as I said it, I knew Harry wasn't in the same league as these guys; compared to them he was strictly small time. Rizzo had crossed the room and in the dim light I could see him standing with his hand poised on the door handle. It looked like our meeting was at an end. He handed me a little card embossed with his name and telephone number, Ricardo Valentine, printed in fancy italics. Just do what you can, Johnny, he said, opening the door. I know I can rely on you. I walked out the door and heard it shut behind me.

Harry wouldn't agree to what Rizzo wanted, that was a sure thing, and there was no way I was getting involved in a drugs war. I would warn Harry what Rizzo was planning but then I was out of it. I had done my bit getting Carol away from the queer bastard, somewhere safe. The long dark corridor was empty; outside I had to shield my eyes against the daylight. The car had gone, with no sign of Billy or the black guy; it looked like I was walking. Back on the street I asked someone the time: it was ten past nine. Fuck it, they shut the factory gates at nine o'clock. A day's wages lost, and that bastard Rizzo says I owe him. There was no way I was going back to Horace's place; I just didn't want to see Carol. Getting her away from Rizzo had been hard enough; getting her away from me was going to be harder. I was just keeping her hanging on with false hope. It was all over, but now wasn't the right time to tell her. I walked the streets aimlessly for what seemed like hours, before deciding to go home. I knew one thing for certain, I told myself, Rizzo could go and fuck himself; I was out of this whole mess. Shit, it has nothing to do with me, I said aloud.

Chapter Eleven

The house felt like an old friend, safe and comfortable. There was no one home. I put the kettle on and got the biscuit jar from the cupboard. Walking around the old quiet house, it made me wonder why I had left in the first place. Upstairs in my room, I lay on my bed; everything was just as I had left it, and at least they hadn't rented it out. Taking Jill's letters from behind the bookshelf where I had hidden them, I lay back on the pillows and began to read them all. They told me what I already knew, what she knew. I closed my eyes and rubbed the pages across my face, pages that she had touched, pages which said she loved me. I fell asleep, with a happy heart and a new resolve, and dreamt once more of our children.

It was almost two o'clock when I woke up, and when I did I had no idea where I was. My mind was completely blank, no matter how hard I tried. I got up and looked out of the window, and saw the shape of the Vespa under an old sheet standing forlornly on the backyard. And when it all came back, I put it all down to a bad dream; this was my world, the real world. Mum came home just as I got downstairs and put the kettle on. She seemed pleased to see me, never mentioning Carol or where I had been for the past couple of months. She kissed me on the cheek and stepped back to look at me, still holding my arms. Look at you, look at your hair. I don't know, you could do with it cutting. Your dad never told me you had long hair. Mum, will it be all right if I stay awhile? I started to say. This is your home, sweetheart, you never have to ask, she said. Thanks Mum. Kettle's boiled; do you want a cup of tea? I was out in the yard trying to get the scooter to start, so I could go and meet Jill when she came out of work. Have you cleaned the plugs? Dad said from the back door. He came over and knelt down beside me. Your mum says you're staying. Only if that's all right with you. Don't be so bloody stupid, he said, putting his hand on my shoulder; just don't go upsetting your mum. I shook my head that I wouldn't. If you got back with Jill, now that would please her. I had never known him be so talkative, but it was nice. Yeah, it would please me too, Dad. I'll see what I can do. I think this thing is well and truly knackered, I said, giving the scooter a kick. Go and ask Barry to take a look at it; I'm sure he can fix it, Dad said, and your mum says to tell you your tea's ready. Barry wasn't in, so I covered the scooter up again and walked across town to meet Jill.

The five o'clock whistle blew, and they all came streaming out like the crowd at the end of a football match. In my five o'clock world when the whistle blows, no one owns a piece of my time; it reminded me of the old

Vogues song. *The bloke who wrote it must have worked in a factory*, I thought, as I sang the words. From my view standing across the road, I was afraid I would miss her. Then suddenly there she was, the most beautiful girl in the world; she was arm in arm with another girl, deep in conversation. I walked along following them from my side of the road, waiting for the other girl to leave. The crowd had started to thin out when it occurred to me that her friend might be with her all the way home. Crossing over, I walked behind them for a little while, until I could wait no longer. Jill, I said, putting my hand on her shoulder and making her jump. She turned around. Jesus, you almost gave me a heart attack. I had been worried in case she might not want to see me, but the way we just stood and looked at each other gave me this strange feeling that only ever happened when I was with her, and I just knew she had the very same feeling. She was still wearing her factory apron, and I wondered why she had given up her education for this. She would never be a factory girl if I had anything to do with it. We had forgotten about Jill's friend who was still hanging on to her arm, we were so wrapped up in each other. You go on, Karen, Jill smiled at her, I'll see you tomorrow. Karen seemed reluctant to go. I can wait for you if you want, she said. Just fuck off, Karen, I wanted to say; instead Jill said, No it's okay. See you tomorrow then, Jill, Karen said, giving me a dirty look before slowly wandering off into the darkness. Anyway, what are you doing here? Jill smiled, and she really did look pleased to see me. I was just passing when I saw you from across the street. Liar, she said, taking hold of my arm as we began walking slowly.

I didn't think I'd see you again, she said after we had walked in silence for a while. Why, what made you think that? I asked her. She stopped and turned to look at me: Because of what you said. I said a lot of things, Jill, and most of them I meant, but I couldn't stand not seeing you again. Shh, she said, putting her hand across my lips. I breathed in the familiar scent of her skin through her fingers, and if that had been my last breath I would have died a happy man. While I was lost in these thoughts she took her hand away, and moving closer she kissed me. I tried to think back to the last kiss, while people walked past and the traffic blurred into a mirror of headlights. I returned her kiss as we stood in this wondrous place. We held hands and walked ever more slowly as we got nearer to Jill's house. It was so comfortable that I began to imagine we had never broken up: there was no Rizzo, no Carol, no cunt of a boyfriend; I still could not call him by his name. When her house at last came into view she led me into a bus shelter; we stood in a corner kissing and keeping each other warm.

Your hair's really long, she said, pushing it back behind my ears. I think it suits you. Do you remember that? she said pointing to a place on the wall: JB LUVS JW was printed in black marker pen, amongst all the other graffiti. Yes I do, but is it still true? I said, pulling her close once more. She started to giggle. At home I've still got my pencil case and ruler with your name written all over them – I love Jonty – and yes, you know I do. Then why are you still with him, Jill? I don't get it. She buried her face against my shoulder. Why are you still with her? she sighed. I'm not;

it's all over. She studied me closely for a moment. Why? she said; was it because of me? Destiny, Jill, remember? I smiled. Destiny, she repeated, it's inevitable. What did your mum and dad say, when you told them about the baby, I suppose it's okay because they think it's his. I haven't told them, I heard her say. You haven't told them, I repeated. She shook her head no. Well, that's good, I said, kissing her hair. What's good about it? she wanted to know. Don't you see? I said, sounding excited, I can come home with you now, and we can tell them we are going to have a baby and get married?

Just hold on, Jonty, please, she started to cry; you make it sound so easy, she sobbed. It is, Jill; let's do it. She kissed me, and I swallowed her salty tears. I've got to go, she said, suddenly pushing herself away from me. She went outside and walked across the road, before she ran back and kissed me. I'll wait for you outside work tomorrow, I called after her as she crossed the road again. She turned and waved. See you tomorrow, I said again.

Walking back home I went over all the things we had talked about, and convinced myself that we were together again. We would soon be married, with our own place and a baby. Well, I must say you look happy, mum said. She was laying the table for dinner, the smell of home cooking in the air. I had forgotten how good home-cooked food was, in the months I had been away. Go and tell your dad dinner's ready, she said. He was sitting in his chair reading the evening paper. Everything all right? he said, putting the paper down. I knew what he meant, and I wanted to tell him that Jill and me were back together. Everything's fine, I said. At that moment I felt so close to him, with the urge to hug him and tell him how much I loved and admired him, but I didn't know how. Uncle Jack turned up after dinner, and the three of us went down the road to the Railway for a pint. We stayed till closing time, and put the world to rights. On the way back home I stopped at a phone box and rang Carol. Where are you? she sounded worried. I told her Mum was ill so I was staying the night. I miss you, she said. You too, I lied. Johnny, I haven't taken anything all day. That's great, Carol, I'm proud of you. Listen, I'll see you tomorrow. I'm scared, she said, they might come looking for me. Carol, they don't even know you're gone. Anyway, you're safe with Horace. I'll see you tomorrow, I said again. I love you, she said, as I put down the phone. I felt awful but what could I do? I just couldn't come straight out and tell her that it was all over between us.

I was waiting again across the road from the factory gates, the next day. Karen was coming across to me. She was alone, and that old familiar sinking feeling returned once more. Hiya, she smiled, looking happier than she had any right to be. How could she be so nonchalant? My whole fucking life could come apart at any moment. I could see an envelope in her hand, but she made no attempt to give it to me. I stared at it, imagining what it said. Jill went home early, I heard her say. Oh, I said, still staring at the envelope. She was feeling sick, you know, sick from the baby, she said, when I didn't reply. Is that for me? I asked her, unable to stand it any longer. What? she said. The letter in your hand; is it from Jill? No, she laughed, it's just a Christmas card from someone. I felt stupid, but I suddenly remembered what she had just said. Feeling sick was only natural when you were pregnant; this wasn't the brush-off after all. Listen, thanks for letting me know, Karen. I'll probably call and see her later on, I said, starting to walk away. She's not really sick, Karen suddenly blurted out; she just said that so she could go home early and get ready for tonight.

Tonight? I repeated, my puzzled look reflecting in Karen's eyes. She suddenly lowered her gaze, and we stood in an awkward silence. All around us life went on, people and cars moving by, until it seemed as though we were the only ones moving and everything else had stopped. You don't know, do you? I heard Karen say, and I put my hand out to stop her from moving. I can't do this, she said, not seeming to notice my hand on her arm. It's her hen night tonight. I looked at her blankly, as though she had been speaking in some foreign language. She's getting married on Saturday. I'm so sorry, she added. Don't be, I said, smiling at her; it's not your fault. Are you all right? she asked me sounding genuinely concerned. She was all right. Thanks for telling me, Karen. Do you think I'll get an invite? I said, trying to put on a brave face, which wasn't fooling anyone. See you around, I said, walking away. You won't do anything stupid, will you? Karen said behind me. I was aware of her watching me; in fact it felt like the whole world was watching, and most of them laughing.

So that was that. Fuck her, the bitch; he could have her, was my first thought as I walked away. Was it only twenty-four hours ago that we were walking down this very same street, holding hands and declaring undying love for each other? And there lay the answer right in front of me; she loved me; it was all I needed to know. There were reasons for what she was doing: she was pregnant, and her head was all over the place, but most of all she was being pressured into this by that fucking evil bitch she had for a mother. Suddenly things didn't seem so bad after all. Hadn't we been down this road so many times before and always ended up back in each other's arms? So what if she was getting married to someone else? All I had to do was wait; it wouldn't last, it couldn't: no one could stop destiny.

I was going to go home, but now I had a new resolve in me as though I had found some hidden strength. Changing direction, I made my way to Horace's. I had to finish this whole thing with Carol once and for all. I couldn't keep putting it off, waiting for the right moment, or I would be waiting forever; now was the time.

There was no answer when I knocked on Horace's front door; in fact the house was in complete darkness. There was no way they would have gone out. Carol was laying low just in case Rizzo sent someone looking for her. Rizzo, fuck, I had forgotten all about him and what he had asked me to do; the deadline he had given me was long gone. I walked around the back of the house and tried the door handle: it was locked. There had to be a simple explanation for this, I tried to convince myself, but I had a bad feeling. I tapped on the kitchen window and called out their names, but there was no reply. Looking around in the darkness for something to break in with, the kitchen light came on, catching me in its glare. Horace appeared at the window; Jonty, is that you? he said. Open the fucking door, Horace, I said, showing myself to him.

They came for her, Jonty. I didn't tell them honest, Jonty, I didn't tell them, the words rushed out of Horace's mouth before I had stepped through the door. It's okay, Horace, I said, shutting the door behind me. What's happened? Where's Carol? Two men came looking for her; they had guns. She saw them from the window and hid upstairs. I told them she wasn't here, but they didn't believe me. They broke my fingers, he said, holding up his right hand. His first three fingers were blue and swollen, the joints all distorted; he looked like he might pass out at any moment. She came down when she heard me scream. I didn't tell them, Jonty, honest I didn't, he cried. What did they look like, Horace, these two men? Was one black, and the other one, did he have a broken nose? Yes, that's them; do you know them, Jonty? Who are they? Shall we call the police? Where did they take her, Horace? Come on, think. Did they say anything? I shouted at him. No, I just heard the black guy say, come on, you've got to go back to work. The flat – they had taken her back to the flat.

Horace gave me the keys to his car, but they had left nothing to chance: all the tyres had been slashed. I called a taxi for Horace, with instructions to take him to hospital, and set off running to the flat. Riding up in the lift, it occurred to me that if Rizzo's heavies were still there, what the fuck was I going to do? Calling the police was out of the question, because no matter what, I was involved. The lift doors opened and everything seemed perfectly normal. I put my ear to the door of the flat –

there wasn't a sound. My heart pounding in my ears, I slid my key into the lock and slowly turned it. When the door was open about six inches, my imagination running wild, I pictured someone waiting behind the door. Throwing my weight into the door I swung it wide open, crashing it into the wall. The place was in darkness. Without a sound, I shut the door and reached for the light switch. My eyes scanned the room – everything seemed fine… then I saw her. She was kneeling on the floor in front of the fireplace. Christ, Carol, what the hell are you doing in the dark? I said. Halfway across the room I stopped. She was dead. Her face had turned a bluey grey colour, and thoughts of the kid in the car with half his head missing came flooding back. She was icy cold when I touched her face; I drew my hand away in horror. I knelt down on the floor facing her and put my hand under her nose and in front of her mouth just in case; a single teardrop fell onto the back of my hand, making me jump to my feet.

There was a syringe still sticking out of her arm; it hung limply down, pulling up the skin around it. I started to reach and pull it out but stopped myself; I couldn't afford to get involved in this any more than I already was. I sat back down on the floor. What sort of shit had she put in her body? I thought as I sat and looked at her. Carol was dead, and I felt like I should be crying, but no tears came. Truth be told, I was feeling relieved: she was out of my life now, no longer my problem. What a heartless bastard I was. What the hell was I doing sitting here? There was nothing I could do for her now. I needed to get away. I got to my feet and headed for the door. Then it suddenly hit me. I walked back and knelt down in front of Carol again. Jesus, somebody had killed her. Not somebody – this was Rizzo's doing. The needle hung from her right arm; it was the only mark there. Her left arm bore all the telltale little red marks and tiny scabs of her habit. Carol was right-handed; she couldn't inject with her left hand. The bastards had given her a massive overdose. The cops would think it was just another junkie shooting up for the last time. Just like I had for a little while. Rizzo had had her killed; she was no use to him anymore. Was it even my fault for not doing the little favour he had asked?

My mind raced with all these theories: maybe he was watching the flat, and the cops were speeding over here right now to catch me with a dead hooker. Remembering what they always did in the movies, I found a pair of rubber gloves and a duster under the sink. All the while listening for the siren of an approaching cop car, I cleaned the apartment of any sign of my existence. The bloke with the white powder and the little brush would find fuck all. The wardrobes were nearly empty; all of Carol's clothes were at Horace's. A couple of Fred Perry three-button polo shirts that Carol had bought me sat on the top shelf still in their packaging. My football holdall was under the bed; the caked-on mud that clung to my football boots had dried to a brittle powder that gave off little wisps of dust that smelt of better days when I chucked the shirts on top of them. I went from room to room; there was not a lot to show for two lives. The most important thing in the apartment was my record collection, which had been left here to collect later and take straight home. I took the holdall in to the front room to put the records in; the record player was there but there were no records. Whoever had killed Carol also had a love of music; some bastard had nicked my records. I was ashamed to realise that I was more upset about losing my records than losing Carol.

Sitting on the sofa I stared at the empty space under the record player. Out of the corner of my eye Carol knelt on the floor like a stone statue. Visions of Horace's broken fingers came leaping into my mind. What the fuck was I going to do? I couldn't go home and tell my dad. Dad, I've been living with a junkie hooker, but someone's killed her. The only certain thing was, I was on my own. The cops obviously weren't coming, and it was no use me ringing them. I don't think they would think much of my murder theory. My first instinct had been to run and keep on running, and I probably would have, but things had changed. Rizzo had had Carol killed, and I felt partly to blame, and one of the killers had stolen something of mine. Rizzo was going to pay; how, I didn't know, I would work that out later; first I had to get out of this mess.

There was no way I could just leave Carol; it could take days or even weeks before anyone found her. The thought of what she would look like if she was left to rot sent a shiver through me. Carol had never mentioned her family; if she had any brothers or sisters I didn't know. The only person she had talked about was the actor bloke, just an image on the silver screen. There was a phone box on the corner opposite the apartment block; I decided to ring the cops from there. Still wearing the rubber gloves, I picked up my holdall and took one last look around the apartment. Outside, the hallway was empty; I closed the door behind me without looking back. Taking the fire escape stairs so no one would see me, I left a life behind with every step. I dialled 999 and some bird asked me which service I wanted. A girl's taken an overdose. I think she's dead. You say she may have taken an overdose, sir. Do you know what of? the girl asked me. What the hell did it matter if she was dead? I thought. Look, just get an ambulance and the police. I was about to hang up, when I heard her say: What address, sir? I gave her the address. Could I have your name, sir? I heard her say as I put the phone down.

The Ship and Anchor pub was just around the corner on the main road; the cops and the ambulance would have to come past this way. I went in and sat by the window with a pint and waited. The ambulance turned up first, no flashing lights, no sirens wailing, and no fucking hurry, twenty minutes after I had made the call. The cops followed five minutes later, so I drank up and went outside. Already quite a crowd had gathered, mainly women and kids on bikes, huddled against the cold night air. They've found a dead body, one old dear said as I walked casually by. I heard it's murder, said the woman next to her. See, I told you, she added, as another police car pulled up. Right, let's have you moving on; you've all got homes to go to, a fat sergeant said, moving towards the front entrance. No one left to go home. Go and fetch your dad, one woman said to a kid on a bike. Leaving them to their morbid speculation, I walked away, worrying about my indifference as the kid on the bike peddled furiously by.

Horace was sitting in the dark; he came to the door when I called through his letterbox. Where's Carol? he asked, when I stepped through the door alone. It's okay, Horace, they won't be back, I told him, snapping on a table lamp. His broken fingers were taped together, a bottle of painkillers by his side; he looked terrible. Where is she? he asked again. There was no easy way. She's dead, Horace, I said, putting my arm around his shoulder. He said nothing for what seemed an age. Did they kill her? he said at last. No, Horace no one killed her, it was an overdose, an accident. I couldn't tell him the truth. Tomorrow's papers would tell him the same thing, at least that was what Rizzo was relying on. I was sure it was a safe bet; only Rizzo and the two blokes who had injected her knew what had really happened. I knew of course, but there was nothing I could do about it. Horace wept silently, and I wondered why I didn't. What are we going to do, Johnny? he said through his tears; what are we going to do without her?

I woke up the next morning free of Carol with not a trace of guilt and put it down to being in shock. Everyone at work was in a holiday mood, and they let us finish at dinnertime as we were breaking up for Christmas. Nearly everyone headed for town to get pissed or see if they could pull. Usually I would have done the same but I had something else to do. On the way home I bought the early edition of the evening paper; halfway down page three I found what I was looking for. Just a small paragraph of a few lines: police were called to an apartment building last night in the Parks area of the city. The body of a young woman was found; she was pronounced dead at the scene. A police spokesman said they were not looking for anyone else in connection with the death. The identity of the young woman had not been revealed at the time of going to press. So that was that, Rizzo had got away with it. Just a few lines in the paper cleared him, and to my relief cleared me. All day I had half expected the boys in blue to feel my collar and haul me in for questioning, shopped by some nosy old busybody. But thinking about it, to the cops Carol was just some sad junkie who had taken one fix too many. I threw the paper in a litterbin and went home.

Chapter Twelve

I decided to have another go at fixing the bike. The plan had been to sell it, have some driving lessons and buy a car, but somehow I had got lost for those three months. Pulling back the tarpaulin I was surprised to see how good the bike looked. It felt good to sit on it again. After nearly an hour of cleaning the plugs and taking bits and pieces off the engine, the fucking thing still wouldn't start; fixing it was beyond me. I remembered what Dad had said about asking Barry to have a look at it, so I went next door but one and knocked on his door. Barry was a greaser, at least he had been until he got married. He seemed to spend all his spare time tinkering around with his motorbike in the backyard. He had a 650cc Norton, which he said he had gone 125mph down the dual carriageway on. Oh hello, his wife said, opening the door. Hello Mrs Graham, I was wondering, is Barry in? I asked. No, he's not back from work yet, John, but he should be home anytime now, she smiled. A little girl appeared from behind her mother's legs; she looked half asleep, her blonde curls framing her face. She tugged at her mother's skirt, shifting her pink dummy from one side of her mouth to the other with a sigh, two little streams of snot running from her nose. Her mum bent down to pick her up, giving me an eyeful of her tits.She took the dummy out of the little girl's mouth. Say hello to Johnny, Angie; come on, sweetheart, don't be shy. Angie gave me a crazy smile that revealed a gap where her front teeth were missing. I think someone's been kissing the boys, I teased her. She was a cute little girl; Barry was a lucky man: a good-looking wife and family. While I was giving her the once-over, I noticed the slight swelling in her belly. She must have seen me staring. Almost four months, she said. Thoughts of Jill and our own unborn baby raced through my mind. Barry is a lucky man, I told her, and she gave me an embarrassed smile.

Just then the Norton came roaring down the road. Well, if it ain't mod boy, Barry grinned, killing the engine. He took off his helmet and pushed his long hair behind his ears. I thought you'd left the country or something. I haven't seen you in ages. No, I haven't been around much. I was living somewhere else but it didn't work out. So you're back home. What happened? Did she dump you? he smiled. Yeah, something like that, I shrugged. Barry got the Vespa running within half an hour; Fucking Eyetie shit, he said, listening to the engine ticking over. Take my advice, and get rid of this piece of junk while it's still running. Yeah, I know, that's what I intend doing, I told him. Mind you, I suppose they're just right for you ponces, little girly bikes like this, he laughed. Fuck off, that thing of yours can't be much better, it's always in bits and pieces all over the back yard, I said. That's just fine-tuning, mate; just a tweak here and there makes all the difference. He looked at me. You don't know what the fuck I'm talking about, do you? he said. I shook my head no. Take it for a long ride, he said, and it should be okay. Thanks, Barry, I owe you one, I said.

So you've been shacked up with some bird. Did she throw you out, or did you get fed up? he asked. What happened to that pretty one who was always round here? It wasn't her, was it? he said without waiting for me to answer. Jill. No, it wasn't Jill, the sound of her name on my tongue suddenly taking me to some other place. You're a lucky fucker, love 'em and leave 'em, mate, I heard him say through my thoughts. Don't make the same mistakes as I did. I gave a little laugh. What's funny? he said. It's just that I was only saying to your missus what a lucky sod you are. He looked at me to see if I was winding him up. How the hell do you make that out? he said. Well, look what you've got: a wife and a little girl and another baby on the way; you're settled with a lovely family. Me, what have I got? Sweet fuck all. Fuck all, he laughed, I wish I had fuck all, out every night a different girl, getting pissed; you're as free as a bird, Johnny boy, don't wish your fucking life away. Free and single ain't all it's cracked up to be, Barry, believe me. Fucking hell, she really got to you didn't she, mate? Go and see her, go and sort it; she's obviously worth it.

Barry, your dinner's on the table, his wife called from the backyard, and from within the house Buddy Holly sang

Words of Love: Hold me close and tell me love is real, tell me how you feel. Great track, I said. I thought you Mods liked all that Soul shit, he said, looking surprised. Not me. Give me Buddy Holly any day, I smiled. Have you got any of his albums? he asked. I did have but some bastard nicked all my records. You're kidding, who would do that? Oh, I know who did it; he had my girlfriend murdered too. He looked at me in astonishment for a moment. Fucking hell, you had me going there for a while, he said, laughing. You are having me on, he added. Yeah, just kidding, Barry.

The snow that had been threatening all day started to fall in tiny flakes, sticking to whatever they landed on like a fine white powder. It was fucking freezing but it still felt good to be on the road again; the bike seemed to run better than I remembered it ever running before. The streets were still packed with the lunchtime revellers, just coming out of the pubs to make their way home. There seemed to be girls everywhere, most of them half pissed and acting stupid. They were queuing out of the door and round the corner at the chippy. I spotted Sue coming out with another girl who I didn't know. Jonty, stop! she shouted, seeing me at the same time. I pulled up across the road. They were both eating chips, and neither of them could walk straight as they tottered across the street. A car came around the corner and had to do an emergency stop. Sue and her mate didn't even seem to notice. The driver rolled down his window and said something to them. Sue gave him a V sign and threw a handful of chips at the car as it sped off. Twat, she slurred, in the direction of the car, breathing beer and chips all over me. Where the hell have you been? Everyone's been asking about you. Do you know what's happening tomorrow? she continued without waiting for an answer. If you mean the wedding, then yeah, I know all about it. She stopped eating and peered at me closely. How do you know? she said. Are you going? I asked her, ignoring the question. Course I am, are you? she giggled. No, I didn't get an invitation, unless it comes in the morning. She's making a big mistake, he's not right for her. What are you going to do about it, Jonty? Wait, I said, shrugging my shoulders. That's so romantic, and so sad, the other girl said. We both turned to look at her. Well, I think it is, she said. So where have you been hiding all this time? Sue asked. You don't want to know, Sue, trust me. Have you seen Roothy lately? I asked her, changing the subject. Probably in Borstal by now I shouldn't wonder, she said. You're joking, aren't you? I said laughing. No, he was at court today. Why, what's he done? He punched a copper when he was pissed. Fucking hell, I said to myself. Maybe I had let him down; he was my best friend, and I wasn't there for him. Funny thing is, I saw him last week and we got talking and it was really nice, just like when we first met. Maybe it's my fault he's like he is, she said, echoing my thoughts. Her eyes had started to fill with tears. Come on, Sue, it's not your fault.Roothy's one of the nicest blokes I know, he would give you his last penny, but when he starts drinking, I don't know, just something comes over him and he changes into someone else. I feel sick, she said, handing me the rest of her chips.

I think you should go to see her get married, Sue's friend said. You could sit on your scooter outside, and when they come out, you could rev your engine and then burn off down the road. It would be just like Jimmy Dean and Pier Angeli. Who? we both said together. She looked at us as though we were idiots. James Dean and Pier Angeli she repeated. God, she's beautiful. Anyway, she married this other guy, some singer, just because her mother told her to. Fuck, I knew it, I said aloud; that's just what's happening to us. She didn't love this bloke she married, she loved Jimmy, the girl continued. Exactly the fucking same, I said, shaking my head; I was starting to like this girl. Come on, Judy, don't leave it like that; what happened? Sue demanded. Honestly, don't you know anything? Judy sighed. It didn't last. He started hitting her ,and they split up. You know you look a lot like James Dean, Judy said, staring at me intently. Her stare was beginning to unnerve me, until she suddenly shivered. Someone's just walked over my grave. Now, that's weird, she said mysteriously. Did he have her back, this Jimmy bloke? Sue wanted to know. No, Judy said, staring at me again, he couldn't; he was dead. No happy ending there, then, Sue said, sounding disappointed. Judy suddenly seemed in a hurry to leave. Come on, Sue, it's freezing standing here, she said, linking her arm through Sue's and pulling her away. Hey thanks, Judy, I called, starting the engine; maybe I will go tomorrow after all. Then I remembered I didn't know where she was getting married or at what time. Hold on a minute, Sue, what time is it tomorrow and where is it? I thought you knew, she said smiling. I don't think I should tell you. Fucking hell, Sue, come on. If I tell you, promise me you won't cause a scene, cause I know you, Jonty. Honestly, Sue, cross my heart, I just want to be there, nothing else.

I rode around aimlessly for another half an hour and then headed back home. The snow had just about stopped, leaving a thin white dusting on the ground. It swirled up in the bike's wake and settled back down again as though it had never moved. The late edition of the paper was lying on the table when I went in. Nothing had changed since the earlier one; it was still the same report. The thought of Rizzo reading the same thing and laughing started to get to me. I should have been frightened of him and what he could do, but I wasn't. I lay in bed that night and thought of Carol lying on some cold mortuary slab all alone. I couldn't let Rizzo get away with it, I had to do something. Fuck it, I told myself, wrestling with my conscience; I had been lucky once, I had to stay out of it from now on. Every moment had to be focused on Jill.

Saturday morning was cold and frosty, giving the snow an artificial glaze; in the sunshine it reminded me of sugar icing. Jill was wearing a pink suit, her hair tied back with pink ribbon; she was carrying a small bouquet of pink flowers in her hand. She looked so beautiful, but so sad, so lost, and on the path of sugar icing, like the little bride figure on top of the cake, except she wasn't in white. Even from across the street I could see the tightness of her skirt against her gently swelling belly. She saw me straight away; she knew I would be there. Mrs Brown fussing around her daughter followed her gaze. Her fixed smile slipped for just a moment, and her eyes willed me to leave. The disgrace of a registry office wedding was almost too much to bear. Her only daughter knocked up, dressed in pink instead of white. The smile returned to her face, and I almost felt sorry for her. There were maybe twenty people around the bride and groom, showering them with confetti and taking photographs, but she never took her eyes off me. The strange thing was, right at that moment when she had married someone else, I loved her more than ever. Revving the scooter, I roared away down the road just like Jimmy Dean. Who the hell was Jimmy Dean? I laughed like a crazy man, I don't know if anyone noticed.

Christmas Day wasn't too bad; we had a house full for dinner. It was great playing with my eldest sister's two kids and being called uncle. Well, this makes a change. Is this the new you? My sister was sitting on her husband's lap watching me play with the kids. No, it's still the same nasty me, I said, pulling a face. Listen, why don't you ever come around to see us, we never see you, and you could bring your girlfriend. That's a laugh, you know I don't have a girlfriend, I smiled sarcastically. Did you know Jill got married yesterday? she said. Yeah I know, I was there. What, you went to the wedding? she said, sitting up. Well, I didn't exactly get an invite, but I watched from across the road. Oh, she said, and it didn't bother you? I looked at her. What do you think? I'm sorry, she said, I always thought that you and her were made for each other.

The day after Boxing Day I took the scooter out and rode around all the local churches, reading all the noticeboards for any information of Carol's funeral. There was no shortage of customers, but I couldn't find Carol's name on any of them. It slowly dawned on me that I knew absolutely nothing about her: where she came from, who her parents were. Maybe that was the answer to why I couldn't find her name; her home could be in another part of the country. The only one I could think of who really knew her was the actor, and I didn't have a clue how to get hold of him. Then I remembered that Harry's brother was an undertaker; he would know how to find out where the funeral was. I would go down there tonight.

It was early when I got to the Derwent that evening. It was pretty quiet, only about a dozen people in. I walked across the dance floor; four girls were dancing to some shit Motown record. Harry was behind the bar polishing glasses. He looked up when I leaned on the bar. Johnny boy, he greeted me with a huge smile, where the fuck have you been hiding? It was nice to see him after such a long time, and nice to be back in the old Derwent where Roothy and me had had some great times. Carol had never wanted to come here; she'd said it was full of spotty little pretend Mods listening to crappy Soul music. It suddenly occurred to me that it was almost in this exact spot where I had met her surrounded by pretend Mods listening to Soul music. What had she been doing there, and if she hadn't been would she still be alive? Are you still living with that sophisticated bird? Harry asked. No, not anymore; actually, that's why I'm here, Harry. He put a pint of lager in front of me. Get that down you; on the house, he smiled. Who's the DJ? I asked him, as the young kid behind the decks dropped his next record on the floor. Harry gave me a look that said don't ask. I don't suppose you'd fancy coming back and doing Sunday nights for me, he asked. I almost said no, but then I thought why not? I didn't exactly have a full diary in front of me. Okay, I don't mind helping you out, Harry, I said. That's fucking great, Johnny, just one thing don't bring that lunatic mate of yours – he's too much trouble. Harry obviously hadn't heard about Roothy's court appearance. I hope they lock the little fucker up, was all he said when I told him. They did, Harry; he got three months in borstal, I told him. Oh, he said, looking shocked. Listen, what I just said, I didn't mean it. Neither of us spoke for a while. Harry busied himself behind the bar while I flipped a beer mat and watched the dancers.

So you were saying there was something you wanted to ask me, Harry said, breaking the silence. Yeah, is your brother still an undertaker? I asked him. He stopped wiping the bar and looked at me. Yeah he is, why, have you got him a customer? Something like that, only I don't know where or when the funeral is, and I thought maybe he could find out. Who is it? he asked. Who died? Carol, I said, Carol Connelly. He looked at me for a moment. Carol, he said; isn't that the name of that bird you've been shacked up with, the actress? She's not an actress, her boyfriend's an actor; anyway, she's dead. Harry sounded shocked. How? he asked. Drug overdose. At least that's what the police think. Someone killed her Harry; they gave her some bad shit, fucking murdered her. You are pulling my leg, he said with a nervous laugh. No, I'm not, I said, shaking my head. I knew she was trouble, I knew it, he said to himself.

I wish I was pulling your leg, but it's true they had her killed, and I'm partly to blame. Everyone works for the man, Harry, except you and me. I don't know what you're talking about, Johnny. Who the fuck's the man? Harry said. Have you heard of a guy called Rizzo, or Ricardo Valentine to give him his real name? Yeah, I've heard of him, Harry said; he owns three or four clubs in the city. Well, I think he might want this one, I said, sweeping my arm around the room. You can either work for him, or if you don't then he'll just take it. Harry just looked at me in disbelief. Don't look so worried, I said, I think the heat might be off. I explained to him the favour Rizzo had asked me to do, about Harry selling Rizzo's stuff in his club, and how I hadn't done it and as a result Carol was dead. You don't know for certain that he killed her, Harry said, sounding desperate; it might have been an accident if she was on the hard stuff. You're right, Harry, I don't know for certain, all I'm saying is watch your back. He disappeared around the back of the bar, and I wondered if I had done the right thing in telling him. Why I hadn't done it in the first place, God knows. If I had then might Carol still be alive? The funeral's New Year's Eve at eleven o'clock, Harry said, coming and sitting next to me. She's down at Allen's Funeral Parlour till then. I thanked him and got up to leave. Can you do New Year's Eve for me? Harry asked. I'll make it worth your while, he added. Yeah, sure I will; only trouble is, some cunt's nicked all my records. Harry took his wallet out and gave me two tens. Here, get some more, he said, smiling. At the door I turned to see him deep in conversation with the suits. I thought about going back to tell him that Rizzo's goons carried guns but it didn't really matter anymore.

The following day I walked down to the funeral parlour to see Carol. My part in her death had started to get to me.

I was glad I was out of it, out of my relationship with her, but not at the cost of a life. I wanted to get even with Rizzo; just what the fuck I was going to do I had no idea. But just suppose Harry was right, it could have been an accident; maybe this murder theory was all my imagination. All these thoughts ran through my head as I walked through the streets.

A scruffy old bloke let me in when I knocked on the door; he motioned me in and went and sat behind a desk and picked up a dirty magazine that he had obviously been looking at. For a moment his appearance threw me. I had been expecting someone smartly dressed in a black suit and tie. Carol Connelly, I said, at last finding my voice, I've come to see Carol Connelly. He looked up from his magazine. I thought you might have, he said. He pushed his chair back, the noise of the steel legs scraping against the stone floor echoed around the room. Enough noise to wake the dead, he laughed. This way, he said, walking past me; he still held the magazine in his hand, open at the centre spread of a blonde with enormous tits. Across the room he stopped before a red velvet curtain. A tenner, he said, holding out his hand. I looked at him, not knowing what the hell he was talking about. What? I said. You get to do whatever you want; you can fuck her if you like. What the fucking hell was he going on about, fuck who? I seemed to be missing the point somewhere. You're not related to her are you, the deceased that is, he asked me, cos I was only joking you know? The young lady's in there; he held the curtain open. Beads of sweat stood out on his high forehead even though it was icy cold in the room. No I'm not, I said, stepping past him.

The room beyond the curtain was narrow and windowless, more like a corridor than a room. She lay against the end wall, with just enough room for a chair at the side of the table where she lay. I thought she would have been in an open casket, something to make her look less vulnerable, instead of being laid on a cold steel slab covered by a thin cotton sheet. Someone had got her makeup all wrong; she looked like a sad clown. I sat down beside her and looked around the room; the only other thing in it was a bunch of plastic flowers hung with cobwebs. I still couldn't find anything to say to her. The truth was, I wasn't that bothered. I mean, I'd never even shed one fucking tear. The only thing that bothered me was Rizzo, and the fact he had got away with killing someone. What was it with death and me? It seemed to follow me around. *Fuck this,* I thought, getting up to leave, *I shouldn't be here.* The old bloke looked up from his magazine as I approached him; he looked as though he couldn't decide whether to do a runner or not. Then the penny dropped; his reaction suddenly explained to me what he had been talking about earlier: he was actually selling necrophilia.

I should have felt horrified and appalled, but the irony of what Carol had done for a living, and was now doing in death, made me smile. Look, what I said before, don't get the wrong idea, his voice trailed off as I stood over him. Do I look like I'd want to fuck a corpse? I said. Well, probably not, but you never can tell. I get 'em in here all the time, he said, warming to his subject. Oh yeah, they drop by regular just to see who's in, he said, jerking his thumb in the direction of the back room. That's why I lay them on the table; it's hard to fuck them in a coffin. He must have thought he had gone too far, for he suddenly backtracked. It's a terrible job sitting here alone with the dead but someone 'as to do it, he said, as though that made everything all right. Have many people been in to see her, I asked him. You mean relatives or, he said, pausing to look at me. Relatives, I said. None, he said, shaking his head; no one's been to see her to mourn her and say what they have to say. He waited for me to say something. That's why I thought you might be, you know, he said at my silence. Maybe I am, I said. I knew you was, he smiled; after so long in this job you get a feeling about people. How many fucked her, then? I smiled at him. Just a couple, but it's a nice little sideline; the job only pays peanuts. What about you? I asked him, still smiling; a perk of the job for you, you lucky bastard? He started to laugh, Oh yeah, I always get to go first, especially when we get someone young and pretty. Well, thanks anyway, I said, turning to leave. Oh, by the way, there's something you should know before I go. She was a whore, I nodded in the direction of the curtain; more prick than you've had hot dinners, and she's got the clap.

Chapter Thirteen

The frost had given way to an almost muggy feeling that hung thickly in the morning air; the clouds overhead were the colour of slate, so low in the sky that it looked as though all you had to do was reach up your hand to touch them. Halfway there, a fine misty drizzle began to fall, the fine drops of rain clinging to the shoulders of my suit jacket like tiny drops of mercury. It took me less time than I thought to get there; I looked around for a suitable vantage point out of the rain. Across the road from the church a clump of five or six spindly trees stood at the top of a slight rise. Leaping the low stonewall I walked up to the trees, the hard ground beneath my feet getting softer with every step. I leaned against a tree and looked at my watch again, waiting, wishing I hadn't quit smoking; I could have murdered a fag.

The church stood strong and defiant, blending in to its surroundings until it almost disappeared. I blinked my eyes until it came back into focus; it seemed to be staring back watching me, sending a shiver through my body. The sound of an approaching car came as a relief, and turning my head I watched an old Rover 90 slowly come into view. The car continued past the church and turned into the narrow lane at the side, parking on the grass verge. The sound of the creaking car door opening rolled across the hillside, and an old man stepped out and looked around him. He was wearing a cream mackintosh, from the pocket of which he took a pipe and put it in his mouth, making no attempt to light it. From where I was standing he looked a bit like Harold Wilson, but I couldn't think of any reason why the Prime Minister might be here. A thought suddenly occurred to me that he could be a cop, a detective, although maybe he was a little old. I watched as he walked around to the front of the church. He stopped to read the little wooden noticeboard that stood by the side of the gateway. Maigret, that's who he reminded me of. Suddenly another car appeared from nowhere, shattering my thoughts. A shiny new silver Jag shuddered to a halt right in front of the church gates, spraying pebbles in every direction, its slipstream whipping up the edges of the notices posted on the board. Maigret put out his hand and held them down, turning to look at the driver who was now stepping confidently out of the car. Rizzo strode through the church gates past Maigret and down the path, disappearing inside the church as though he were late for his own funeral. The fucking nerve of the bastard, attending his own victim's funeral; was he trying to prove he had a conscience? The old bloke stood and watched him, making no attempt to take out his handcuffs and arrest him, so I came to the conclusion he was no cop. But what bothered me more was Rizzo. What the fuck was he doing here, a killer with a conscience?

I began to question my own motives for being there; plain and simple, a guilt trip that was supposed to make me feel better about my total lack of any feelings for Carol. Across the road the vicar had appeared from the darkness of the church. He stood with his hands clasped together in front of him; it was probably the only way he knew. Every few seconds he cast a nervous glance over his shoulder. A black man alone in his church – what was the world coming to? Even from where I was standing it was obvious that the vicar's doctrine of We are all God's Children, had gone out of the fucking window. The old bloke with the pipe was walking towards him through the headstones, and the vicar ran to meet him like a long lost brother. Only two more turned up, one of them a young woman wearing a smart black suit, her blonde hair reminding me of Mary and another funeral. After Mick had died, I had told myself that that was it with funerals: I wasn't going to any more. Nothing had happened to change my mind, until I saw Rizzo that is. I had arrived with no intention of actually going into the church, but now wild horses couldn't stop me. I wanted him to see me; I wanted to show him I wasn't scared of him. The bastard certainly wouldn't be expecting me; he probably thought I had fled the country. Fuck it, he still had something of mine, and I meant to get it back.

The pall-bearers, well rehearsed, slid the coffin out and hoisted it on to their shoulders like soldiers at drill on the parade ground. When they were halfway down the church path, I jumped over the wall to follow them. Just at that moment another car pulled up, a swanky two-seater MG Sports with a soft-top. The driver killed the engine and jumped out, almost in one movement. There was no mistaking him, although he looked much smaller than I expected, but the last time I had seen him he had been in wide screen and about thirty feet high. Our eyes met as I crossed the road just behind him, brushing dried mud from the bottoms of my trousers, and just for a fleeting moment a slight smile played across his face. We followed the sad procession through the gravestones, me still a couple of steps behind. He had a way of walking, which he had obviously refined; it was somewhere between John Wayne and Robert Mitchum. Actually, it was quite impressive, and I thought of trying a few steps myself.

Inside the church I looked around for Rizzo; there he was in the front row. I should have known. I started to walk towards him, fully intending to sit right next to him, but I decided to leave the surprise until later. Taking a seat near the back, I looked around at the mourners scattered about haphazardly like wind-blown parachutes. Even with the pall-bearers and the old lady who gave out the hymn books, it was a pitiful sight. Someone somewhere surely must have loved and cared for this girl; she had to have had a mother and father. The thought that perhaps they didn't know, happily carrying on with their lives, unaware that today was their daughter's funeral, made me wish I had shown more of an interest in her life. The realisation that I knew hardly anything about her was not made any easier by the fact that she hadn't wanted me to know anything. The vicar seemed slightly on edge with Rizzo so close, keeping one eye on him throughout the service just in case he pocketed the collection plate, or stripped the lead from the roof. It was all over in ten minutes There was nothing to say, no one to tell him what sort of person she was, what kinds of things she liked. Taking his eyes off Rizzo for a moment he looked around hopefully: there were no takers. I glanced across at the actor – the stage was all set for him – but he stared blankly ahead, lost without a script. So the vicar reluctantly led us in a final hymn. We stood with our heads bowed while they carried her back outside, and I wondered if she would be buried or burnt, and who would be paying.

Rizzo was following the pall-bearers, his head down as though he were grieving. Hey Rizzo, how you doing? I said to him as he walked past. He looked up with a start, and I swear he turned pale when he saw it was me. I winked at him, and getting himself together he flashed me a gold-toothed smile. Outside I watched him hurry to his car and drive away. The drizzle had stopped and watery sunshine made weak shadows on the ground. Excuse me, I called after the actor as he walked past. He stopped and turned around. I'm sorry, but I don't think now is the right time to be asking for autographs, he smiled. What? I laughed. I don't want your fucking autograph. Oh, he said, looking disappointed. I was starting to like this guy, he had real style. No, I just thought there were some things you should know about Carol.

The four of us stood by the church gates and watched the hearse until it disappeared around a bend in the road.

For a moment we stood in awkward silence: the old man, the young woman, the actor and me. The old man said he was her friend; how he knew her he didn't say. He was almost certainly one of her clients, I thought, but then again what did I know, she fooled me for long enough. I can't believe she's gone, the old man kept saying, dabbing at the corners of his eyes with a handkerchief.

At that moment I decided to keep Carol's secret just that. The young woman's name was Grace; she was a nurse, who had done her training with Carol. Carol was a nurse? the actor and I both said together. She looked surprised that we didn't know. How did you know Carol? she asked the actor. I didn't, he said, well, not really; we had spoken on the phone quite a lot. Wait a minute. Are you saying that you never met her? I asked him. No, not face to face, only on the phone. You didn't live with her? I mean, wasn't she your girlfriend? Girlfriend? he repeated, sounding confused. No, she was my fan club secretary. Whatever gave you that idea? Nothing, I think I got hold of the wrong end of the stick, I smiled. What about you, he asked me, what was your relationship with Carol? I knew this question would be coming, but suddenly I didn't know what to say. Yes, how did you know Carol? I heard Grace say. They stood looking at me hopefully, so I told them the truth. I'm an old boyfriend, I heard myself say. Old boyfriend? Grace mocked. Surely not that old, Grace said. You're so young. She took me to the pictures once to see you in a film, I said, turning to the actor and ignoring Grace's remark. She was so much in love with you. I could feel Grace looking right through me. That's nice to know, the actor said, which one was it? Which one what? I said, sounding like some idiot. Which film did you go to see? he said. Oh sorry, you know I can't remember what it was called, but I remember you snogging this dead fit bird, and you get paid for it. He laughed, It's not that easy, especially when you have a wife. Fuck, he was married too. I wondered if Carol had known. Well, it's been nice meeting you all, the actor was saying, I'm just sorry it was in these sad circumstances. He seemed in a hurry to get away, and it occurred to me that maybe Carol could have been telling the truth. *Why don't you get on his case Miss fucking Marple?* I thought, glancing at Grace. He shook hands with the old man and me, and kissed Grace on each cheek the way actors do, and with a wave of his hand he turned and made his way to his car in that super cool way of walking. Even if he was lying, he was in the clear, the dead can't talk, but who was I kidding? He wasn't lying. The only liar here was me.

Grace insisted on giving me a lift back to town. I didn't want to go. I knew she was looking for answers, and I knew she thought I had them. She wouldn't take no for an answer. In the car she kept sneaking sideways glances at me. There's something you're not telling me, she said eventually. It was a good job Grace was a nurse and not a cop, I thought.

I don't know what to tell you, Grace, there's so much I've learnt about Carol today; in fact, we could all have been talking about a different girl. Was she in some kind of trouble? And who was the black man I saw you speak to at the church? She seemed determined to find some little thing that was wrong. Carol worked for him, his name's Rizzo, and everyone works for the man, I said, smiling to myself.

We were back in town. Anywhere, here will be fine I told her, anxious to get out of the car. She pulled over into the side of the road. What exactly was Carol's job? she said, turning to face me. I couldn't tell her the truth, so I told her what I had believed for so long, that she had had an important well-paid job in some big organisation. This Rizzo, she worked for him, you said. Yeah that's right; he owns bars and nightclubs everywhere. What about the drugs, where do they fit in? Carol would never even take an aspirin when I knew her. The truth would have been so much easier, but I couldn't bring myself to tell her. Like you just said, Grace, when you knew her; people change you know, I said, opening the door. I felt her hand on my arm. She died a junkie, a drug addict; doesn't that bother you? she persisted. What do you think, Grace? Maybe you think I'm a junkie too, do you? I'm sorry, really I am, but she was my friend, and you're so young. I don't know what to think. Just go home, Grace, and remember all the good times you and Carol had together. Don't think about things you're not sure of; sometimes it's better not to know.

You remind me of Icarus, she said. I looked at her blankly, who? Icarus flew too close to the sun. Just be careful: you might get burned. I smiled at her, I'm truly sorry about Carol, she was a beautiful lady. She grabbed the sleeve of my jacket and pulled me back inside the car. What's your star sign? she asked me. Sagittarius, why? She sat in silence for a moment. Just be careful, she said again.

Her expression had changed and fear came through her eyes, and just for a second I felt really spooked. Shit, she was as bad as my mum, every day reading the stars in the paper; in fact it was the only thing she ever read, that and *Rebecca*. Thanks for the lift, I said, and remember, too much thinking is bad for you. Stay safe, she said, giving me a sad smile. Fucking mumbo jumbo crap; across the street a ladder leant against a shop front. I hurried across the road and walked under it, fuck it. I caught my reflection in a shop window; I looked really cool walking down the street in broad daylight in my suit. All the bad shit was nearly over; things were going to get better, I told myself.

Chapter Fourteen

New Year's Eve found me playing records again at the Derwent; it felt good, almost as though I had never been away. Looking out over the sea of bodies packed onto the dance floor reminded me of better days, although most of them were a new crowd. So much had changed in the space of a few short months: Roothy was locked up, Carol was dead, and Jill was married. Everyone was high, but I was even higher, even though I hadn't taken shit. Harry had got the word that Rizzo's boys were going to show tonight. Since I'd told him about Rizzo's proposition he had become paranoid. For at least the tenth time he came up to ask me, Any sign yet? Relax, Harry, nothing yet, I reassured him. He was relying on me to point them out; even though the suits were posted all over the place, none of them knew what they were looking for. I slipped The Rockin' Berries', *The Water Is Over My Head* on to the turntable; fucking Tamla Motown was giving me a headache. You certainly know how to clear the dance floor, someone said. I looked up to see Moira standing before me like a beautiful apparition. Most of the blokes were heading to the bar, and the girls left on the dance floor stood around looking vacantly at each other.

They don't know a good song when they hear it; this is a classic, I smiled at her. How are you? she said, leaning in close to make herself heard; I haven't seen you in ages. The scent of her long hair that brushed my face made me wonder what might have been if Roothy hadn't fucked it up. She looked worried, concerned, and I wondered what she knew, what everyone knew. I'm fine, I smiled, even better now I've seen you. She gave me a shy little smile. I bet you're not on your own, are you? She shook her head. No I'm with my boyfriend; that's him, she said, turning around, the one leaning against the wall in the black jacket. I followed her gaze; he looked all right but she could do better I thought. Some blokes have all the luck, I told her. What? she said. I didn't hear you. Watch this, I said, putting on *My Generation*. If they don't dance to this they can all fuck off. Moira called her boyfriend over. His name was Tony, and he said that he did a bit of deejaying, which gave me an idea. Tony was going through the records at the side of the turntables. I wouldn't have dared play that last record, he said. Why not, it's better than all this Soul shit, I said, casting my arm over the boxes of records. Who was it anyway? he asked me. You don't know who that was? I smiled at him. You know who this is though, don't you? I said, looking at the dance floor packed again. Everyone singing, talking about my generation, my generation, why don't you all fuck off. Course I fucking do, he laughed. I would have played *Jump and Dance* by The Carnaby but some thieving bastard had nicked it. Instead I put on *boom boom boom boom everybody fall down* by The Applejacks – fucking ace! The fact was, Harry's money had bought me a Who album, two Buddy Holly albums and a load of 45s, and all the Soul records I had borrowed off Rastus. Listen, Tony, would you do me a favour and sit in for me while I go for a piss and get myself a pint? I asked him. Do you mean it? he said, his face a picture. I moved out from behind the decks. It's all yours. You better play some Tamla Motown though or there might be a riot. I left him to it to go and find his girlfriend, but something stopped me dead.

Fucking hell, I couldn't believe it, Billy was standing at the bar, cool as you like. I'd know that bastard anywhere. I looked around to see if I could see any more of Rizzo's goons. Which one is he? Harry said when I told him. Is that all? He's only a bit of a kid, he laughed when I pointed him out. Billy was making his way through the crowds towards the toilets. Harry signaled a couple of the suits, and we followed. Inside the toilets on the far wall by the Durex machine, Billy had quite a crowd gathered around him. It was obvious that he had been here before; everyone knew him, and they didn't care where the gear came from, Rizzo or Harry. What the fuck's going on here? Harry's voice echoed around the tiled walls. Most of the crowd scattered as Harry pushed his way across the room. Billy and another bloke stood with their backs to the wall like rabbits caught in the headlights, only with no place to run. Billy held a flight bag in his hand with more pills than Boots in it: the other one had a fistful of money. You backstabbing little fucker, Gordy, Harry said. How could you do this to me? It's not how it looks, Harry, honest I can explain, Gordy whined, looking like he might piss himself at any moment. I kept my eye on Billy. He might be a problem; I knew what he was carrying under his jacket. And just who the fuck are you? Harry demanded, turning his attention to Billy. Me, I ain't nobody, Billy said, trying to keep his cool. I was just buying stuff off him like everybody else. Looks like you bought the whole fucking lot, Harry laughed, grabbing the bag off Billy. Is he one of Rizzo's boys, Jonty? Harry said, turning to me. Billy followed his gaze, and when our eyes met, I saw the spark of recognition and the hate I had seen before. Billy's right hand moved slowly across his chest, towards the inside of his jacket. Stepping forward I grabbed his wrist, and a couple of the suits pinned him back against the wall. The gun nestled in its fancy leather holster, and when I held it in my hand it felt like a lead weight for something so small. Billy seemed to shrink before my eyes, as though with taking his gun away I had taken his heart. He looked close to tears, and I almost felt sorry for him; neither of us was cut out for this life, and I wanted to put my arm around him and tell him just that.

How the hell had he got into all this? How the hell had I? Gordy and Billy leaned against the wall staring down at the floor. A couple of lads walked in, saw what was happening and walked back out. So, Harry, what are you going to do with these two? I asked him. Harry pondered the question a moment; he looked pretty vacant standing there stroking his beard. Shoot the fuckers, he said with a nervous laugh. I was still holding Billy's gun. I held it out to him. Do you want to do it or shall I? He recoiled in horror at the sight of the gun. Poor old Harry was just playing at gangsters, the trouble was Rizzo was for real. Throw them out, he said to the suits. Hey you! Harry grabbed Billy as they led him out. Just tell your boss this is my club and fucking sending little boys with guns doesn't frighten me. He shook Billy's arm. You got that sonny? he said. Billy's old swagger was beginning to come back a little at the realisation that he wasn't going to be shot, or have the shit kicked out of him. Yeah, I got it, he sneered, but you better watch your back, granddad, and you as well, ponce, he said, grinning at me. I raised the gun and pointed it at him, and everybody ducked. See you, Billy, I said, as they hurried out of the door. I stuck the gun in the waistband of my jeans.

Harry tipped the contents of Billy's bag on to his desk: boosters, purple hearts, black bombers, French blues, nigger minstrels spilled out, popping across the desk like jumping beans. Help yourselves, lads, he said. I reached over and scooped up a handful, stuffing them in my jacket pocket. Well, Jonty, so much for your mate Rizzo, Harry said, looking pleased with himself. I think we sorted that black fucker out. I said nothing, but I had the feeling that this was just the beginning of some all-out drugs war that Harry couldn't win. Outside the door I swallowed a couple of black bombers without even thinking; old habits die hard it would seem. Back in the bar Tony seemed to be enjoying himself, and the dance floor was packed, every record sounded the fucking same, but they seemed to be enjoying it. I suddenly missed Carol, missed talking to her about music – she'd taught me so much. How was I going to get my records back, my Glenda Collins singles, my French Who EP, the Vogues single that I had nicked, and fucking *Kelly* by Del Shannon, the best Bside ever? Moira was waving at me from the dance floor; I motioned her to come over. What do you think you're doing with my boyfriend? she frowned, looking really mad. I'm sorry, Moira, I was just going to… Her face broke into a smile, and she burst out laughing. I think you've lost your job, she said. Yeah I know, he's a natural. I took her arm and guided her towards the bar.

I got Moira a Babycham and Tony a pint; don't go away, I'm just going to take him this drink, I said to her. This is fucking great, he laughed when I handed him his pint. Are you all right for another half an hour? I asked him. Only I need to see someone. Say no more, mate, you take as long as you like, he said with a knowing smile. If only he knew what I had in mind, I thought as I walked away.It was nearly half past eleven; Tony would still be playing records while I would be kissing his girlfriend at midnight. Back at the bar I told her he wanted me to look after her for a little while longer. She looked at me with a look that said I know exactly what you're doing, but it also said I don't mind. It looks as though he prefers playing DJ than spending time with me, she said. Well, he must be an idiot, I told her. I bought her another drink, brushing her hand when I handed her the glass. She smelt wonderful, all clean and brand new. At the first stroke of midnight I held her in my arms and kissed her; the bombers had begun to work, and I suddenly felt alive again. *In The Midnight Hour* was on the decks, drowning out the chimes of the old year: Tony's idea of being a smart arse. Even while I kissed her, thoughts of New Year's resolutions ran through my head, speeded up by the pills. My head felt like it might explode. The need to see Jill was so overpowering, and somewhere at this very moment I knew she was feeling exactly the same. I think I love you, Moira said, her head resting on my shoulder. I think I've always loved you. I should have put an end to it right there at that very moment, instead I kissed the top of her head, and through the crowded floor I caught a glimpse of Tony and felt no remorse.

We arranged to meet in a couple of days, after she had let Tony down gently. Back behind the decks I played The Cryin' Shames' *Please Stay* and watched them leave hand in hand. I put The McCoys' *Hang on Sloopy* on for the last record, Roothy's all-time favourite, the only record he would dance to. Swallowing a couple more pills I made my way to the dance floor. I danced like a spastic just like Roothy, to the amusement of the crowd. Fuck it! I shouted, laughing like a madman.

The gun clattered onto the floor at my feet as I undid my jeans. I stared at it for a few seconds and then looked around the room to see who had put it there. Fuck, suddenly it all came back; the effects of the pills were wearing off, and the reality of my involvement stared me in the face. I flushed the rest of the pills down the toilet; they were just like everything else, they didn't last. Back in my room I picked the gun up from the floor, and stepping in front of the wardrobe mirror I raised it at arm's length, pointing at my reflection. Sitting on the edge of the bed I examined the gun on my lap. Fucking hell, the gun was loaded; the shiny brass bottoms of the bullets stared up at me. That Billy was a real headcase. I hid it on top of the wardrobe between a stack of old football programmes.

Two days later I was waiting for Moira at the bus station, hoping she wouldn't show, hoping for the easy way out. What did you tell him? I blurted out as soon as she stepped off the bus. Please tell me you didn't go through with it, my mind was saying. She took hold of my hand. Come on, she smiled, let's walk. This is all I've ever really wanted. So many times I've imagined this moment, just walking along holding your hand. She was beautiful, sweet and kind. What the hell had I been thinking? I was just caught up in a moment. She deserved better than me. What is it, I heard her say, why are you sighing? I wasn't, I smiled at her; I was just thinking I don't deserve someone like you. I decided there and then that I would give it a try, but in my heart I knew it was hopeless. Where women were involved, I was just a weak bastard. We walked the cold frosty streets, stopping to look in the shop windows, and when we got too cold we sat on the warm steam pipes in the bus station. I wrapped my scarf around her, and we walked some more, kissing in dark shop doorways. Walking along with our eyes raised to the sky, counting the stars, laughing as we began to wander all over the place as though we had just stepped off a fairground ride. Standing on the old wooden bridge, we peered over, waiting for a train, and sat on the freezing cold platform sharing chocolate from a machine. Fuck I was trying, but I realised with a heavy heart that all we had done was all the sacred things that me and Jill had shared so many times before. When I didn't see Moira, I rode the scooter past Jill's house; back at home I stayed in my room playing the few records I had. I made up my mind to pay Rizzo a visit and get my collection back. The expected backlash from New Year's Eve hadn't happened and now a month had nearly passed. My time with Carol seemed like a distant memory, almost like she had never existed, and when I slept I dreamt of Jill, and now when I awoke I remembered every dream.

Chapter Fifteen

It was the first week in February, a warm spring-like sun shone down from a cloudless sky, a Saturday morning I would always remember. I saw her across the street coming out of a shop, and she was alone. I sprinted down my side of the street about fifty yards, and then crossed the road and began to walk towards her. As she drew closer I could hear my heart pounding in my chest. Hello Jill, I said, my voice strangled somewhere in my throat. Hello Jonty, she smiled, it's really good to see you. Behind her smile, she looked drawn and sad, and there were dark circles under her eyes. I had always thought pregnant women were supposed to be a picture of health. I had not seen her since her wedding day six or seven weeks ago, when even from across the street I could see her gently swelling belly. Now she hid her pregnancy under a baggy man's jumper. I couldn't bring myself to ask where her husband was. How long now for the baby? I said instead. Two months, she said, two months too long. You are all right, aren't you?

I mean you and the baby. She looked like she might cry. No, I'm fine, we are fine, she said, pulling herself together. I was sorry to hear about your girlfriend; that must have been terrible, she said, changing the subject. She wasn't my girlfriend, I said defensively, not when she died anyway; we had already split up. There was no way I was going to go into detail about Carol. Fucking hell, Jill would never have anything more to do with m,e even though I hadn't done anything wrong.

Do you want to go across the road to the Kardomah and get a coffee? I asked her. Yes, she said, taking me by surprise. We sat upstairs by the window, and she told me everything, about her fucking husband walking out after only three weeks. Jesus fucking Christ, all those weeks ago and I didn't know, all that wasted time. Why didn't you tell me? Why didn't you let me know? You've got your own life, Jonty, a nice girlfriend; you don't want my problems, especially after the way I've treated you. She reached across the table and took hold of my hand. The touch of her hand, the feel of her fingers gripping mine, almost made me want to cry. I looked around the room in the hope that everyone was watching us, everyone was looking at me holding hands with the most beautiful girl in the world. We talked non-stop for an hour, our coffees untouched and forgotten. She tried to persuade me to stay with Moira, to live another life. I don't love her, Jill, I love you, and this time there's nothing standing in our way. She made me promise to give it a month to think about everything. I couldn't see anything to think about but I agreed, and we promised to see each other once a week. Let her down gently, she said, as we said goodbye. We kissed out on the street on a busy Saturday; there was nothing to hide.

You're quiet, Moira said; what's wrong? Nothing, I said, smiling at her. I should have been kind, I should have been a man and told her right there, told her that I was in love with Jill. Whatever it is, it's all right, she said, squeezing my arm. I remembered how she had looked at me on New Year's Eve when I had wondered just how much she knew. The answer was she knew everything; she knew I was in love with Jill. I pulled her close and kissed the top of her head. Everything's fine, I told her. We sat in the Duke and put our money down for table football, and spent the rest of our money playing *I Want You* by The Troggs, and *Wonder Boy* by Lesley Gore, over and over again on the jukebox.

At work on Monday someone told me that the Derwent had burnt down during the night. The rest of the day I wondered how we could have all been so stupid, so stupid thinking that Rizzo wasn't going to come calling. It was inevitable really; there was no way of stopping it. As soon as I had clocked off at work, I hurried across town to the Derwent. Harry was alone, standing before the blackened ruins of his life, his club, our club. I stood and watched for a while, feeling uneasy about invading his privacy. Puffs of smoke spiralled skywards every now and then, and as I approached him, he reminded me of Maxim de Winter, standing before Mandalay. He glanced at me when I stood by his side, and neither of us spoke. It's still warm, he said after a while, raking his foot through the ashes. Can you feel it? Fucking hell, Harry, I'm sorry; we had some great times here, and you can build it up again. He turned to look at me and shook his head. No insurance, he said. That bastard Rizzo, one day he'll get what's coming to him. The fire bloke said it was probably an electrical fault, and the cops aren't interested; what do you think, Jonty? What did I think? I didn't think anything. I didn't want any part of this. Who the fuck is he anyway? I mean, I've never even seen him, he's like some fucking ghost,.Why would he do this? Harry said. Because he can, Harry, and believe me he could do even worse. So that's that then. I just accept what he's done, destroying my livelihood. What did he want me to say? Just leave it, Harry, it's over; do something else. He said nothing but I could see the disappointment in his eyes. I'm sorry, Harry, I said again, walking away, turning to look back at the last rays of the sun shining through the blackened ruins. Mandalay came to mind again. *Rebecca* came to mind again. It was all Mum's fault: she had read the book so many times she knew it word perfect and so did I – she still reckoned he got away with murder.

Two days later and I still had the picture in my mind of Harry standing before what was left of his burnt-out club, totally distraught. Rizzo was still laughing, still the man, the untouchable man. Carol was dead, poor innocent Horace had had his fingers broken, and Harry had been put out of business, all for not working for the man. Like it or not everything was connected to me, and I just couldn't leave it alone. Now was the time to pay Rizzo a visit. The Who's album *My Generation* had been playing non-stop for the last couple of hours, and I felt ready for anything. I was going to get back what was mine. Standing on the bed, I took the gun from its hiding place and sat on the edge of the bed looking down at it in my hand, the bullets in the chamber glistening in the light from the beside lamp. Fuck it, it's not true, it's not true, I'm telling you, cause I'm up here and you're nowhere, so there. I turned the record player off.

Walking through the dark streets, I could see where Billy got his bottle from: the gun was everything, armed and dangerous, and no wonder he was always looking for a fight. The place looked so different in the dark, the drab red brick building illuminated in flashing neon lights, and for a Wednesday night it was busy. At least a dozen scooters were parked out front, and a group of Mods stood around the entrance. Keeping to the shadows I made my way down the side of the building to the car park at the rear. The thought suddenly occurred to me that Rizzo might not be there, after all this wasn't the only club he owned. But the Jag I had seen him driving at Carol's funeral was parked at the bottom of the iron fire escape, I went up the steps two at a time, this time of my own accord, this time with the gun. I rang the bell that had sounded so loud before, but Otis Redding belting out *I Can't Turn You Loose* downstairs left it sounding faint and far away. There was one of those little spy holes in the door; I looked right at it, imagining Billy staring back on the other side. After a couple of minutes the sound of a bolt being pulled back came from inside. The door opened a few inches, held there by a chain. Yeah, what do you want? the face peering through the crack said. I've come to see

Rizzo, I said, trying to recognise what I could see of the face. You got an appointment? he said, looking me over. Appointment, I laughed. I've come to see the man not the fucking doctor, I said sounding like somebody else. Who is it, Jonah? I heard someone ask from behind the door. Some little pillhead Mod wanting to see the boss, Jonah said over his shoulder. The chain slid back, and the door opened wide, the huge figure of Lenny filling the frame. Well, look who it ain't, he beamed. I was wondering when you might turn up. Come on in, Jonty.

This was it; once I was inside anything could happen. The thought of what he had done to Carol should have made me turn around and leave, instead I stepped through the door feeling the muzzle of the gun under my shirt pressing into my skin. The bare red lights stretched down the long passageway, looking for all the world like a ghost ship. Is he here, Lenny? I asked him; is the man here. Oh yeah, he's here, and I'm sure he's got time for you, pretty boy. Just you wait here a minute, and I'll go and tell him you're here, he said. Lenny disappeared into the gloom of the passageway, while Jonah eyed me suspiciously. I looked at him looking at me; he was about the same age as Billy but he had no class, no style;, that was one thing about Billy, he knew how to dress. Something suddenly occurred to me: what if they searched me? In all the films I had ever seen you never got to see Mr Big without being frisked. Jesus, I was done for. What the hell was I going to do? But then again, the last time I was here they hadn't searched me, although then I was in my overalls, armed only with a flask and some sandwiches, not a fucking gun. All these thoughts ran through my head as I waited for Lenny to return. Okay let's go, pretty boy; Lenny was motioning me to follow him. Just a minute, Jonah said, blocking my way, we need to see if he's carrying. Oh fuck; my mind was completely blank and my feet felt like they were nailed to the floor. For a big man Lenny moved fast. Good, Jonah, that's good, you're learning fast, he said, stepping in front of him. Let me do it, he said, standing in front of me. His huge hands moved up and down my body, and when he felt the gun just for a second our eyes met. Okay, he said, turning to Jonah, he's clean. What was happening? Lenny must have known I had a gun or why didn't he let Jonah search me, and why was I now on my way to see Rizzo with a loaded gun? We walked down the passageway together as though we were both on the same side, both working for the man.

Hello Johnny, he greeted me in that posh voice. He was sitting behind the same huge desk, as though he had never moved since the last time I was here. Please take a seat, he said, motioning me to the chrome chair positioned on the other side of the desk. I sat down on the low chair almost touching the floor. Rizzo smiled down at me, happy with his advantage. We sat in silence for a while; Rizzo was attempting to blow smoke rings with his cigar. I could feel beads of sweat running down my body from under my arms, my shirt was sticking to me, and now I was sitting the gun dug into my ribs. I take it this is not a social visit, he said at last. No, you take it right. He laughed out loud and leaned back in his chair. I like you, Johnny, you're not afraid to say what you mean, that's a rare thing these days, a rare thing. You know it's not too late; the offer still stands for you to come and work for me. Thanks but no thanks; like I already told you, I have a job. Perhaps you've come to settle our little debt. I started to speak, but he held out his hand: Forget about it, all debts are settled, he smiled. On the contrary, I've come to collect what you owe me, I said in a calm collected voice. What I owe you? he said, taking the cigar from his mouth and leaning forward, his elbows on the table. What I owe you, he repeated. Do go on, this sounds very intriguing. Just give me my records back, that's all I want. He stared at me looking puzzled. Records, what records? I don't understand, he said. My record collection, which you or one of your goons took from Carol's flat the night you killed her. I hadn't meant to say anything about Carol; all along I had told myself I was here for one reason only: to get back what was mine.

Rizzo continued to stare at me, but his whole face seemed to change before my eyes, and for the first time I felt scared. Ah yes, Carol, he said, a smile suddenly appearing together with the charm he was like a chameleon, a psychopathic chameleon. He got to his feet and then sat down again, putting on a pair of sunglasses. The tiny red beam of light coming from the desk lamp reflected from his shades, giving him the appearance of something from another planet. Such a shame, the poor girl, and what a pitiful turnout at her funeral, he said, regaining his composure. Without the whites of his eyes to focus on he had me at a distinct advantage, staring at some faceless shadow. Johnny, be careful how you choose your words, because if I remember correctly the police said she had died of an accidental drug overdose. No suspicious circumstances, I believe were their exact words. He leaned back in his chair, fading further into the darkness, and put his feet on the desk again, the smug bastard. You had her killed, you fucking murdered her, I heard myself say, sounding surprisingly calm. Well, there's the phone, he said taking his feet off the desk and pushing the phone towards me; be my guest, ring the police. Go on, he urged, tell the police your theory, or maybe I should ring them and tell them that you were living at the flat with her when she died. Should I? he said with his hand on the phone, because you were living there rent free, living there off immoral earnings, in fact; there would be a good case against you for murder: a pimp getting rid of the whore who was doing too many drugs and not enough clients.

I felt for the gun under my clothes and thought about the reason I had come here. I thought not, he said, taking his hand off the phone. You know, Johnny, me and you are not so different. How the fuck do you make that out? I laughed. Well, how did you manage to keep out of all this? he said, taking off his shades. Out of this! I was never in it. I don't want anything to do with what you do, I just want what's mine, I said. You know none of these morons working for me could have done it, he said, not listening to me. I admire you, Johnny, you've got a lot of nerve coming here today, coming here accusing me of murder. He held out his hand: Please let me finish. I'm prepared to overlook all of what's happened; as far as I'm concerned the debt's paid, you don't owe me anything. He sat looking at me as though he had made some grand gesture. You just don't get it, do you? I said, and I thought you were an educated man. Do you think killing Carol was get-even time? I couldn't give a fuck about her; in fact you did me a favour as I was all set to leave her anyway.He shrugged his shoulders. Think what you like, he said, but just remember this: I'm a very patient man but, Johnny, you're beginning to try that patience. What about Harry? I said, ignoring his threat. I suppose you had nothing to do with the Derwent burning down. I think it's time for you to leave, he said, getting to his feet. Look, Rizzo, I'm getting tired of telling you why I'm here. Just give me back my records and I'm gone. He started to laugh: Are you for real? Just get out before I have you thrown out, he said, walking towards the door. I pushed the chair back and turned to face him. Get back and sit down, I said. He turned around and saw the gun in my hand. I watched the expression on his face turn to disbelief and then fear. I followed his gaze and saw I was holding the gun, and for a moment I wondered how it had got there. Now, Johnny, let's work this out, I heard him say. I looked at him: he had his hands in the air, as though he was being robbed, and a nervous smile hung around the corners of his mouth as though he couldn't quite decide what to do. The power of the gun, I realised, was spreading through me. Sit down, I ordered him. He walked stiff-legged back to his chair and sat down heavily, glancing at the door hoping to be rescued. I had a feeling he was in for a long wait. Just give me back what's mine, Rizzo, I said, sitting on the edge of his desk. Honestly I don't know anything about your records, he said, looking over my shoulder at the door again. Nobody's coming, I told him; it seems your staff don't like you much either.

I looked at him shrinking into the chair, and I saw Carol with the needle sticking out of her arm. I saw Harry standing before the smouldering ruins of his club, and I pressed the barrel of the gun against his temple. Please, please, I don't have your records, he pleaded, his eyes nearly disappearing out of the top of his head trying to see the gun barrel. What the fuck was I doing? I was suddenly horrified at myself holding a gun to another man's head. I wasn't going to shoot him. I wasn't a killer. Please, I wasn't even there, Rizzo whined. You weren't where, Rizzo? I wasn't there when she died. It was Lenny, Lenny and Billy, he cried. Lenny killed her, I said to myself. Yes, I heard Rizzo say, but that didn't matter. Suddenly everything fitted neatly into place. I remembered the first time I had met him; he was doing the same thing as me: going through other people's record collections. It was something we had in common, a love of Rock and Roll and a dislike of Soul music, something that I thought made us friends. Lenny had taken my records; Lenny had killed Carol; Lenny who had let me in here knowing I had a gun.

The gun was a heavy weight in my hand, making my arm ache. I felt Rizzo turn his head slightly. How much money do you want? I heard him say. The recoil sent me falling backwards over the desk scrambling on the floor on my hands and knees. I got to my feet and examined the gun still in my hand, my finger resting on the trigger. How the fuck did that happen? I said, looking over at Rizzo. Jesus fucking Christ, half his head had been blown away.

Even in the dim light of the room he was a terrible sight. Rizzo slumped back in his chair, what remained of his head touching the wall behind. Blood and pieces of bone and brain splattered across the wall, looking like some abstract painting.

Behind me someone said, Put the gun down, pretty boy. Turning around I saw Lenny standing with his back to the door. I had never heard him come in. He moved slowly towards me, his hands out in front of him. It just went off, I said to him, holding the gun out to explain. Don't shoot, man, don't fucking shoot, he stammered, putting his hands in the air just like Rizzo. What the hell are you doing? Just take the fucking gun, Lenny, take the gun, I said, turning it around and holding out the grip. He took it from me and went around the desk picking up the lamp and holding it close to Rizzo. Fucking hell, he said. It just went off, I said again; all I wanted was my records. Lenny turned around and looked at me, his face illuminated by the lamplight showing me real fear in his eyes. You killed him, just for that he said, seeing me in a different light, seeing me as some cold-hearted killer. I didn't kill him; it was just an accident; the gun just went off. He knew that I knew he had my records. I could almost see the cogs turning in his brain figuring out what to do next. Fucking hell, I had just handed him the gun. I looked at him, expecting the gun to be pointing at me, but Lenny was busy cleaning the gun with his handkerchief. Don't worry, party doll, he said, sounding as though he had pulled himself together, there's a way out of this.

He knelt down on one knee, careful to avoid the blood gathering on the floor in an ever-increasing pool, and pressed the gun into Rizzo's limp right hand. What the fuck's going on, Lenny? I asked him. He stepped back and looked at Rizzo and then over at me. The fucking black bastard shot himself, right? he asked me. Lenny, you let me in here carrying a gun, why? Yeah, I let you in, man, I let you in to avenge your woman's killing. She's not my woman, she wasn't my woman. I told you I came here for one thing: my records! I shouted at him. You killed for a few records, he said, looking at me in a different way now. We stood facing each other, either side of Rizzo's desk. The music began to drift up from the club below. I could hear Steve Marriott belting out *What's A Matter Baby,* is it hurting you? Hell, what does it matter, he's fucking dead anyway, Lenny shrugged, it don't fucking matter why. Well, you obviously wanted him dead, and I drop right in your lap to do it for you, am I right? I asked him in a surprisingly calm voice. Like I said, what the fuck does it matter? he smiled. It's all right, man, the cops won't be interested in a dead nigger, especially a known villain. What about Jonah? He seemed like a right company man. He could walk in at any moment. I sent him out on a little errand, Lenny smiled; there's no one else here, just you and me. I don't get it, Lenny. How could you know I was going to turn up and kill Rizzo? I didn't, all I knew was that you had Billy's gun, and I got to thinking what I would do in your shoes. I'd probably want to get even. You and me, party doll, we're the same. I knew it when I first met you; we liked the same things, had the same taste in music. Where are they? I asked him; where are my records? How the fuck should I know, man? Hey I know how pissed off you must be but I have no idea where they are. He looked at his watch. Look, Johnny, you got to start trusting me. You've done me a favour; this bastard's dead, and if you hadn't have done it then I probably would have. I owe you one, so when I say you were never here tonight then I mean it; just leave this mess to me. All right? he said, putting his arm around my shoulder and leading me to the door. Hey, this is what I do. I've been cleaning up his mess for years.

Outside the door the corridor was clear. Only the faint sounds of music coming from the club downstairs could be heard; I could just make out Los Bravos' *Black is Black*. From the top of the fire escape doors I could see Rizzo's big flash Jaguar illuminated under a full moon. I felt a shiver run through me thinking about its owner lying upstairs with his brains blown out in a pool of blood, never to drive his car again. Just get on with your life, Johnny boy, I heard Lenny say beside me, it's over; tonight never happened. I started down the steps but halfway down I remembered what he'd said just a few minutes ago, how he cleaned up Rizzo's mess for him. Was it him who killed Carol in his line of work? It wasn't me, Johnny, I didn't kill the party doll, he said before I'd even turned around. We looked at each other for a moment, and I wanted to believe him, but I was fast becoming cynical. He could be on the phone to the cops as soon as I was out of sight. See ya, pretty boy, he called after me as I disappeared into the darkness.

I hurried home, keeping to the shadows. I needed a plan, but I didn't have one. Well, I did: I knew I had to get away, and I mean far away. I was a killer on the run. All my best laid plans literally blown away. Did I actually pull the trigger?

Jesus fucking Christ, did I? I honestly couldn't be sure. What the hell had I become? I thought, suddenly feeling a million years old. There were no cop cars outside our house, only Dad's three-wheeler parked under the street lamp. I went in, and the folks were watching the telly, too engrossed to notice me. Taking the stairs three at a time, I threw a few clothes into my football bag and took down the old tobacco tin from its hiding place on the top of the wardrobe. All my savings were in the tin; I had almost four hundred quid saved towards a car. Mum was always borrowing from it, even though I kept hiding it in some new place, but she always put it back. I stuffed the money in my pocket and picked up my bag. At the door I took one last look at my room, and then remembered Jill's letters. I took them down from the bookshelf and put them in the bag. See you later, I said, going out the front door. Okay, Mum said without turning around; they never even noticed the bag.

An icy wind was blowing down the platform; I sat huddled on an old wooden bench with a one-way ticket to London in my pocket. The café was closed, and a young couple were wrapped in each other's arms in the waiting room. After sitting in there for a few minutes, I stepped outside and sat on the bench, telling myself it was even colder inside than out. The real reason was that they reminded me of my first ever date with Jill, when we had sat in the station waiting room and talked for hours. Jill – she was so close, she was waiting for me, I needed to tell her, write her a letter. I looked frantically about, stood up and searched my pockets, looking for paper and a pen. Where would I get those at this time of night? There was a phone on the platform opposite. I glanced at my watch; the train was due any minute. Fuck it, there was no one about. I jumped down and hurried across the tracks. I was lucky she answered on the fourth ring. Jill, it's me, how are you doin'? I'm fine, she said, the sound of her voice almost breaking my fucking heart. She gave a nervous little laugh. What is it, Jonty, what's the matter? You sound funny. Well, you know me, Jill, always the comedian. Funny strange, dope, she said. Tell me, Jonty, is everything all right? If you've changed your mind it's okay, I understand. Jill, I just called you to hear the sound of your voice. I miss you. I love you. I love you too, she said, and so does little he or she, she laughed. Where are you anyway? That sounds like a train, she said. Behind me the big green diesel engine idled impatiently as doors opened and closed along its brightly-lit body. The pips saved my blank mind; I love you, Jill; speak to you soon. I tore up the footbridge and down the other side, grabbing my bag from the bench and reaching for the carriage door as the guard blew his whistle. Sitting by the window my hot breath fogging up the glass, I peered out, half expecting the cops to come storming down the platform, but there were none. The train slowly rolled out of the station. I sat back and opened the ice-cold carton of milk I had bought from the vending machine on the station platform. Outside, the young lovers emerged from the waiting room. I watched them till they were out of sight. Apart from a solitary trainspotter standing at the very end of the platform writing in his book, the place was deserted. Familiar sights gradually faded away, and I wondered if I would ever see them again. I just prayed that Lenny was telling the truth.

Chapter Sixteen

London, I'd never been to London before. I'd never taken a train journey on my own either; it was past midnight, and suddenly I felt very alone. I took the scrap of paper out of my pocket and looked at the address written on it: Andy Bailey, 15 Lime Tree Court, Islington. Outside the station I got into a black cab and read out the address, and the driver pulled away into brightly-lit streets full of people and cars even at this time of night.

Welcome to the smoke, man, Andy greeted me at the door. His hair rested on his shoulders, and his droopy moustache was now a full-grown beard. Inside, a slim blonde girl with really long legs was lounging across the sofa. Cream were playing on the stereo, and the air was heavy with a mixture of burning incense and dope. Andy had really done it, like I always knew he would. Everyone said he was a dreamer, especially Roothy, but he had done it, moved to London, and right at this moment he was the fucking man. Ingrid was Swedish. Andy introduced her as his flatmate. That's all she is, man, he said when I looked at him knowingly. She handed me the joint she was smoking. Jonty, she said, in a way only she could have said, I like that, she smiled.

The flat was a large Victorian house divided into four separate apartments. Andy's was at the front on the ground floor. What brings you to London? Andy asked me; don't tell me, woman trouble I bet. I told them about Jill getting married and about the baby, and said I just had to get away. That's a bummer, man; I always thought you and her were really tight. I didn't tell them why I was really here, that I was on the run, that I had killed a man just a few hours ago, that Jill was waiting for me carrying my baby, and my girlfriend Moira; I'd never even thought about Moira. What a fucking mess. I didn't tell them any of this. I don't think they would have believed me if I had. Andy and Ingrid told me I could stay as long as I liked; Ingrid had kind eyes that seemed wise beyond her years. When she stood up she looked like a model, very tall, very beautiful, but she worked for the council. Ingrid made me cheese on toast, and at three o'clock in the morning I lay down on the sofa completely exhausted, but sleep would not come, as a million thoughts and images ran through my head. Alone in the dark I cried for what I had done, I cried for Moira who I had let down again, I cried for Jill and our baby who I might never see. Eventually sleep came in the shape of a dream; I dreamt of faceless men breaking down the door and shooting Andy and Ingrid.

Over the next few days I scoured the newspapers and watched every news bulletin on the television. Apart from my daily trip to buy the newspapers, I stayed in the flat and waited for the knock at the door, peeped from behind the curtains at every car door closing. No one came, and there was nothing in the papers; maybe Lenny had done what he said he would do.

Andy worked for the council cutting grass and marking out school playing fields. Ingrid had got him the job. On the Monday of my second week in London, she got me an interview digging graves at Highgate Cemetery, and the following Monday I started work. Spring was in the air, and the weather was kind. Digging holes for the dead was the best job I'd ever had. Every day Ingrid asked me if I had rung Jill. There's something else, something you're not telling me, she said one day after I had once more made some excuse. We were alone in the flat. Andy was out practising with his band The Pulsaters; all his spare time he spent playing his bass guitar.

I can't ring her, Ingrid, something happened and I don't want her getting involved.She sat looking at me for a long while. Whatever it is, it can't be that bad, she said at last. Believe me, it's bad, very bad. Jonty, you're in love with her; whatever it is, she will understand. Two people in love should be together. Ingrid, I can't go back, I killed someone. She burst out laughing. I don't believe you, you could never kill anyone. The silence that followed told her I was telling the truth. I told her the whole story, the whole sorry mess, and when I had finished, it felt like a great weight had been lifted. Ingrid was so sensible, so non-judgemental, listening without making comments, and then telling me how she saw it from someone not involved.

Jonty, it was an accident. Yes, he's dead, but you didn't kill him; a lot of people in your shoes would have. Listen to me, you've done nothing wrong; all you've done is try to help people, and because you've tried to help you're in this mess. But it might not be that bad; all this was a month ago, and no one's come looking for you. Maybe this Lenny is telling the truth. It sounds like there might be a little bit of good in him. Ring her, Jonty, before it's too late, before you lose her. Please, Ingrid, what I've just told you no one must ever know, not Andy or anyone else. She cut me off mid-sentence. Jonty, I thought you knew me; I would rather die than repeat any of what you've told me. Ingrid would be my friend for life; she had given me hope, shown me a way out, something I would never forget.

Mrs Brown answered the phone. When she asked who was calling her tone suddenly changed. Jill's moved out, she said, and you won't find her, she added before putting the phone down. I didn't know if she was telling the truth or not; all kinds of different thoughts ran through my head. Was Jill back with her husband? Maybe they had got somewhere of their own to live. Or was her mother just being a fucking bitch because it was me? There was no one else I could ask; none of my friends had a phone. Over the next week I rang every day, and every time the bitch put the phone down on me.

One Sunday lunchtime, Ingrid and me went to see The Pulsators' first live gig at a pub in Ealing. After a ropy version of *I Can't Explain* they weren't too bad, but Ingrid and me agreed they needed a new singer. There was a phone on the wall between the snug and the bar. After The

Pulsators had done there twenty-minute supporting set, I tried once more to ring Jill. Mr Brown answered this time, and he didn't hang up. Hello John, he said, even sounding pleased to hear from me. Is Jill there? I asked him, I really need to talk to her. He laughed, She's in the hospital. She had the baby last night. Is she all right; is the baby all right? Yes, yes, they're both fine. Is her husband with her? I asked. Look, John, I don't know what's happening with you two, but she's been through a lot, and right now she doesn't need any more upsets. The phone went dead; the bitch had obviously cut us off. Fucking hell, I was a father, we had a baby, and then I realised I didn't know if it was a boy or a girl. The headlining group started up. Andy came over: Was we shit or what? he said. They were playing *Man with Money*; somehow the words seemed prophetic, telling me something. These fuckers are good, I heard Andy say. Yeah they are, I agreed, but they don't have any edge; you lot sound like at any minute everything's going to go tits up, and that's exciting.

That night I wrote my first song; in the morning I left it for Andy, who had packed in his job to concentrate on the band. It was called *That's Just The Way I Am*: That's just the way things are, that's just the way I am, I know you really think so too, it's just a habit saying I love you. The words that ran through my head are the only ones she ever said. They stick like glue inside my mind, pouring from my mouth the cruellest kind, laughing crying living dying, I'm in so deep because of all the lying. I can see her face even though she's not there, something tells me I'll go anywhere, because that's just the way things are she said.

Andy thought it was great; he and the lead guitarist spent the day putting some music to it, and when he played it back on his tape recorder it really sounded quite good. How would you like to join the band? Andy said, catching me by surprise. What, as the songwriter? I smiled. That as well, but we need a new singer, he said, and you've got the looks, Jonty. Fucking hell, Andy, I can't sing, and anyway you've already got a singer. He left, he doesn't dig The Who.Fucking twat, you're better off without him, I said. Too fucking right, Andy agreed, and he couldn't sing either. Inspired by my new role as singer/songwriter, I came up with a song called, *I'm In Love With Carol White*. Really it was all about Jill. They say everyone has a double, and Jill and Carol White could have been mistaken for twins. I played four gigs with The Pulsators, each one more stoned than the last. In that short period of time we became something of a cult band; we were ragged musically all over the place but somehow that was the attraction. The fifth date was cancelled; our lead guitarist overdosed on heroin and was unconscious in hospital. Shades of Carol came back to haunt me, making me realise where I was headed again. I had been away nearly four months. London was fascinating but it wasn't home. Goodbyes are terrible. Andy and Ingrid had been good to me, something I would never forget. The time was right to go home and sort out my life once and for all, even if I got arrested for killing Rizzo, even if Jill had a new life.

The station no longer seemed the dark draughty place I had left that cold night; the summer sun dappled the platform in long warm shadows. Outside, I jumped into a taxi as though I did it every day; London had taught me a lot of things. I gave the driver the address of Rizzo's club; I wanted to get it over with in a hurry, to see if Lenny had been true to his word. Five minutes later I was standing outside looking at a near derelict building, a wire mesh fence stretched across the front of the entrance. Further along the road by the side of a row of shops was a small opening. I squeezed through and came out at the side of the car park separated by a small hedge. Throwing my bag over I scrambled after it; weeds had forced their way through the concrete and were even growing in the guttering along the roof. I walked all the way round the building, stopping at the bottom of the iron fire escape stairs. The door at the top seemed to stare at me, and the thought of what happened behind it made me shiver. My agony would have to go on a little longer. I was going to find no answers here, and I had no idea where to find Lenny.

I made my way home via Jill's house, which was in the opposite side of town to mine. There was no hurry. I had lots to think about. By the time I got there it was early evening. *Fuck it*, I thought, *just do it*. Mrs Brown answered the door; she always fucking did every time I called, like some demented gatekeeper. You're wasting your time, she's not here, she said before I could speak. Actually, it was your charming self I came to see, Mrs Brown, I smiled. Just for a moment my reply threw her, her expression changing to something softer, nicer. She doesn't want anything to do with you, I heard her say. I smiled to myself as her mouth hardened. Just look at you, so full of yourself. I don't know who you think you are. I'm the father of your grandchild, Mrs Brown, just think about that. In the meantime, go fuck yourself, you old bag, I said, walking away. That's right, that's all you can do, you and your foul mouth, she called after me. The moment I had said it I regretted it; telling her to fuck herself was just stupid and childish.

I let myself in, and it was almost as though I had walked out the door only five minutes ago. They were both sat in exactly the same place, watching the telly. The job didn't work out then? Dad said. You should have stayed at the foundry; there was a job for life there. That would have been a short life then, cos I think I would have topped myself, I shot back. Will you two stop it? Mum said, giving me a hug. I was only telling him. I mean, he's not earning now is he? All these big ideas. Mum gave him one of her looks, and he fell silent. Come and sit down, and I'll get you some dinner, Mum smiled. How are you then, Dad? asked me when Mum had left the room. He winked at me and handed me the evening paper, and that was all he said. He was a man of few words and no shows of emotion, but we understood each other perfectly, and I knew he would always fight my corner. I thought back to that night Rizzo died and the two phone calls: one to Jill, and one to my mum and dad via the next door neighbour because we had no phone, calls to the only people I truly cared about. Anyone come looking for me while I was gone? I casually asked Mum while I was eating my dinner. Who would that be then, anyone in particular? She was standing at the kitchen sink looking out of the window. Why couldn't she give me a straight answer? She was always doing that, answering a question with a question. I'd forgotten how annoying she could be. You'd make a good politician, I said. Politician? No, none of them came looking for you, she said, trying to get me to say who I thought would have come looking for me. Pete Townshend, the Queen, the cops, I don't know, anybody, I said. Pete who? she said, taking a seat opposite me. I don't know anyone called Pete. It doesn't matter, Mum, honestly, just forget what I said, I smiled. We sat in silence for a minute. Oh, I almost forgot, Jill came looking for you one day, she said casually. Jill? When? I mean, what did she say? She just wanted to know if you were all right; she said to tell you you'd done the right thing and that she was sorry. Done the right thing, what does she mean? What did you tell her, mum? Tell her? I couldn't tell her anything because you didn't tell me anything; just one phone call, that's all. Did she say anything else? I asked. No, nothing else. It's a pity you two split up; you made a lovely couple.

Chapter Seventeen

Monday dinnertime, I went to the Duke. Roothy was propping up the bar like I knew he would be. Fucking hell, who the fuck cut your hair? It looked as though someone had hacked at it with a pair of garden shears. I ran my hand over his head. They didn't make you wear a suit with arrows on it, did they? He started to laugh: No, it wasn't that bad. When did you get out? I asked him, after I had bought a couple of pints. Last Friday, he said; in the silence that followed I thought back to just a year ago: we were sitting in the same place, laughing, joking, happy and carefree. I couldn't think of anything to say, and I knew it was the same for him. In that year we had both changed, things were different now, and the old times were never coming back, they were lost forever. Have you seen Sue? I asked him. Yeah, I saw her Saturday night; she told me you'd left town and you weren't coming back. Yeah, I got a job in London, but it was time to come back. He looked at me and shook his head. Time to come back to this dump?

Did she say anything about Jill? I said, ignoring his remark. He laughed. I should have known why you came back, but it's too late, Johnny, she's gone. Gone where, do you know? She's living with her auntie or something in Nottingham, I think, that's what Sue said. So the old bag had been telling the truth for once. All I needed now was to find out where in Nottingham.

I needed a job: I needed some money if I was going to get Jill and our baby back; fucking hell, I still didn't know if it was a boy or a girl. For once, luck was on my side; looking through Wednesday's evening paper there was a job working for the local council: ground maintenance, which really meant digging graves. I went straight round there, filled in the application, and twenty minutes later I was offered the job, starting Monday morning. Taking it as a sign that things were going to get better, that night I composed a long letter to Moira, trying the best I could to explain all the reasons she would be better off without me. An hour later I tore it up; it was a bit late to tell her all this; fuck me, it was months ago, she was probably engaged to some nice bloke by now. On Friday night I met Roothy in the Duke, and for a while it was almost like old times, apart from the fact we hardly seemed to know anyone. All the Mods seemed to have been replaced by a new set of faces, noisy and full of themselves but sadly lacking in any sort of passion. Maybe it was me growing older, but even the music was starting to become shite. The night really started to go downhill when Sue walked into the George, which had become the in place while I was away; she was with her boyfriend. Come on, let's fuck off, Roothy said, drinking up. I thought you were over her, man. I thought you two were cool, I reasoned with him. She's fucking loving it, he said, getting to his feet. I'm going to wait outside, otherwise I might deck that bastard, he said, walking away. I was glad he was gone. Just for a minute I thought he was going to start something; a few short months ago he would have. How you doin'? I said, putting my arm around her shoulder. Jonty, she smiled, looking really pleased to see me, where the bloody hell have you been? She put her arms around me and gave me a hug. You look good, she smiled. So do you. Listen, I need to talk to you if you've got a minute. Her boyfriend, who was one of the new faces, had been giving me the dead eye for the last couple of minutes. He put his arm around her protectively. Paul, this is Jonty; Jonty, meet Paul, she said. You all right? I asked him. He looked me up and down, and dismissed me without replying. I need to borrow Sue for a minute, I told him as I ushered her away from him. I nearly said what a twat he was, someone who needed a good fucking slapping, but I stopped myself just in time. He seems all right, I said instead. Do you think so? she asked me, looking as though she didn't really believe me.

Do you know where Jill is? I asked her. Jill ,I might have known; what about my friend Moira? You do remember her, don't you? she said sarcastically. Course I do, I was going to ask you about her, but I thought Jill was your friend. Jill's moved on, Jonty, and so should you, she said. I didn't ask for your opinion, Sue, I asked if you knew where she was. You don't change, do you? That's your trouble. What the fuck does that mean, my trouble? Look, I know

Jill's living in Nottingham. I just want to know where, I don't know honestly, but I wouldn't tell you even if I did. Thanks, that's all I wanted to know, I said, turning to walk away, then I remembered: What did she have? I asked her. She looked at me blankly. The baby, was it a boy or a girl? A boy, she had a little boy. Just leave it though, Jonty, and just get over it. Over her shoulder Paul was approaching with two of his mates in tow. You all right? he said to Sue. He had on a full-length maroon leather coat, two years too late, and his timing was all wrong. *Fuck it*, I thought, laughing to myself, he wasn't worth it. What's funny, cunt? I heard him say as I walked away. I stopped and turned around; all three of them stood in a line, and they all looked terrified. Come on, Paul, let's go. Sue had hold of his arm. Taking a step towards them, the other two moved out of the way just as I thought. Paul was letting himself be led away by Sue. I almost left it but he was just an annoying little prick. I hit him in the gut, and he collapsed to the floor in a heap, Sue still hanging on to his arm. The whole pub fell silent; all eyes on me, the guilty party, as I made my exit; it was great to be back. Roothy stood in the door grinning. She's not worth it, I told him as we stepped outside, you can do better than that.

Work was okay. There were four of us in our section: Jim the foreman, Derek who had been doing the same job for nearly forty years, and young Patrick, a sixteen-year-old Mod. They were all nice, good people; it was young Pat who told me why Rizzo's place was shut down. He was saying how much he missed the Derwent; since it had burnt down, him and his mates had started to frequent

Rizzo's club, until the murder. At the mention of the word murder, I began to get a sick feeling in my stomach. What happened, who was murdered? I asked apprehensively. Oh yeah, I forgot you've been away. Rizzo shot big Lenny, this nigger that worked for him; he was like the doorman at the club; all the Mods used to get their pills from him. Yeah, I know Lenny, but he's not dead; don't you mean Rizzo's dead? I asked him. Yeah, Rizzo's dead, they're both dead; like I was saying, Rizzo shot Lenny and then shot himself. I couldn't believe what I was hearing: Rizzo shot Lenny; how the fuck could that happen, unless I'd imagined that night. The cops reckoned it was some drug deal gone wrong, I heard Pat say. Rizzo was slumped in his chair, his blood and brains running down the wall behind him; he had to have been dead, he couldn't have got up and shot Lenny after I had left. Are you all right? Pat said. You look like you've seen a ghost or something. I smiled at him. Maybe I just did, I said. Fucking creepy job, ain't it? he said, jumping back in the grave we were digging. Well, that was that. I was in the fucking clear, no more looking over my shoulder. I should have been relieved, but it was bothering me. What the fuck had happened after I left? Someone had killed Lenny, but who? Whoever it was, they were walking free just like me.

On the Saturday after my first week at work I caught the bus to Nottingham and spent the day walking the streets, watching the crowds in the city centre, looking, hoping to see Jill. It was useless, I just couldn't think of any way to find her. By the following Friday I'd made the decision to just get on with my life and see where it took me, otherwise I was going to grow old before my time. It was like old times once more, Roothy and me on the town on the pull. His hair had grown to a reasonable length, and he looked like a Mod again. We ended up in the Duke just like we always did; the beer was shit, and the landlord was a tight-arsed git, but they had the best jukebox in town. Gene Vincent's *Baby Blue* hit us when we walked in, Roothy went to the bar, and I put three tanners in all for C 9, The Crickets' *Baby, My Heart.* I studied the titles on the juke, looking for anything new: Johnny Kidd and the Pirates' *Hungry for Love* which was almost four years old, was the latest: fucking ace. We sat in a corner listening to The Crickets, when Roothy nudged me. Look who just walked, in he said. Moira was up at the bar with two other girls; at least Tony wasn't with her. She turned around suddenly and looked straight at me. I smiled at her but she looked right through me. They walked past and in to the snug. What the hell did I expect, hugs and kisses? I sat there and remembered the dilemma I'd been in before I'd left for London; only it wasn't a dilemma: I would have told Moira it was over anyway.

What you waiting for? I heard Roothy say, interrupting my thoughts. I stared at him blankly. For fuck's sake, get in there, she's a fit bird, he said. You are joking. Did you see the way she looked at me, or looked through me? They all do that, he laughed; she just wants you to grovel a bit. I'm not grovelling for no fucker, and anyway Jill might be back. I don't believe you. Jill's gone. You can't wait around for her; she might never come back. For fuck's sake, she might be shacked up with someone else right now. That thought had never crossed my mind, but he was right, no matter how depressing the thought. Come on, let's go, I said, standing to leave. Outside, Roothy looked at his watch. We've just got time for one more across the road at the Nelson. No, fuck it, I'm going, I told him. I'll see you tomorrow. I began to think it had been a mistake to come back; maybe I should have stayed in London. Someone was calling my name. Jonty, wait, she said. I looked back, and Moira was standing on the pavement outside the Duke. When I stopped she started to walk towards me, and I went to meet her. We stepped into a shop doorway and talked. It was like a first date; we were both nervous and excited. Twenty minutes later her friends came looking for her. I'm going to have to go, she said, lightly taking hold of my hand. Will I see you again? I said awkwardly, almost shyly. Do you want to? she asked squeezing my hand. If you're doing nothing, I'm playing football tomorrow afternoon; you don't have to. Where are you playing? she said, smiling, I might just come along.

She turned up just before halftime, just as I was getting worried she had changed her mind. When I saw her walking along the side of the pitch, it reminded me of all the times I used to look out for Jill when she came to watch me play. It was the thrill of seeing her, a feeling of falling in love every time my eyes rested on her face. With Moira that was never going to happen, it just wasn't the same, but Jill wasn't here, and I was weak. At half time I gave her my sweet cup of tea, and it felt good knowing all the lads were looking at her enviously. After the game we walked into town and sat in the window of the Bar L, drinking coffee. Downstairs in the cellar room The Cyclones were playing *Maybe Baby*. Moira had never asked questions, never asked me where I had been, making it easy for me, no lying and excuses. She told me all the gossip, all the things that had happened while I had been away; she told me about the killings at Rizzo's club. What's the matter? she said, in the silence that followed. I smiled at her across the table, seeing the concern in her eyes. I honestly don't know where to begin, I said; it was true, there were so many things bottled up inside. Suddenly they all came tumbling out; I was like a sinner cleansing his soul, which was probably near to the truth. I can't remember what I said to her that day, what exactly I told her, or if she believed any of it. When I had finished talking, it felt as though I had run a marathon, I felt exhausted, tired and weary. We sat there in total silence. I stared out the window, and I could feel her staring at me. It's all right, I heard her say ,stroking my hair, it's all right to cry. Tears were running down my face. I'm sorry, I sobbed, but I've been crying all my life and no one ever noticed until now. She was crying too. I took hold of her hand and pressed it to my face. I'm all cried out, Moira, there's no tears left. I'm fucking cried out.

It was a warm, long summer, and a year had passed since Mick had died, when the end was the beginning; only a year when I seemed to have lived a lifetime. Now there was no Roothy, no Harry; I hadn't seen either of them in months, which for a small town seemed strange. Maybe they were avoiding me, or was I avoiding them? The Mod thing was dying out, and the music seemed sterile and boring, until The Who came up with the "SELL-OUT" album, *I Can't Reach You*, surpassing everything they had done before. Sometimes I thought back to that night when I'd killed Rizzo, but Moira understood and put up with my moods. All the time I thought of Jill, constantly day and night, and sometimes I wondered just how much Moira knew; the realisation that someone could love another despite all of this was a powerful frightening thing. A year gone, a year when everything came together for one brilliant moment and then fell apart. I had lived through it and survived, and just for the times with Jill, good and bad, it was worth it.

We talked of getting engaged, and spent our time looking at rings in the windows of jeweller's shops. I tried so hard to match her enthusiasm, but the commitment just wasn't there. For a time I'd convince myself that this was what I wanted, but I was soon back where I'd started with Moira. This time I was going to have to end it; I just didn't love her.

Chapter Eighteen

September had almost gone, but the wind that shook the leaves on the trees was still warm. We were hanging about that warm September morning, waiting for the graveside service to end. The mourners slowly filed away, except for this really big man in an ill-fitting black suit. He was standing with his back to us, wiping his eyes with a handkerchief. I'd seen this so many times, and each time it really got to me; I was never going to get used to death. I glanced at Pat and Derek laughing and joking; it was just a job to them, like working on an assembly line. The man turned around and slowly began to walk away. At last, Pat said. As he came nearer to where we were waiting I recognised him. Harry, I called out to him. He stopped and looked around, and as I approached him he seemed unsure who I was. Slowly a smile spread across his face. Johnny boy, he said, giving me one of his bear hugs. It's good to see you, Harry, I said, looking up at him. He seemed to have aged ten years in the six months or so since I had last seen him.

Where the hell have you been hiding all of this time? he said, releasing me from his grip. It's a long story ,Harry, I told him. What about you, are you still in the club business? He shook his head: No, after what happened to the Derwent I got out. You know, I really loved that place, he said sadly; still, we had some great nights there, didn't we? he laughed. Fucking ace nights, Harry; remember Roothy's dancing? Fucking hell, he laughed, that was a sight to behold; only trouble was, if he wasn't dancing he was fucking fighting. Anyway, what are you doin' here? he asked me.

The shovel was hidden behind my back, and it didn't seem right to tell him I worked there. Pat and Derek were hovering about behind me, anxious to get on, as it was getting close to dinnertime. Fucking hell, don't tell me you're a fucking gravedigger, Harry said, suddenly catching on. I nodded: Afraid so. That's my mum, he said, pointing back at the open grave. Jesus, I'm sorry, Harry, I didn't know. She was eighty-five and never a day's illness in her life. She was a wonderful lady, Johnny, you would have liked her, he said, his lip beginning to tremble. Look, Harry, maybe you'd like to give me a hand. I brought the shovel from behind my back. He looked at the shovel in my hands; Honest, he said, would that be okay?

We buried her with the midday sun shining down on us, and Harry telling me wonderful stories about her life. When we had finished we leaned on our shovels and looked out from the cemetery hillside to the valley below. Beads of sweat stood out on Harry's brow, his suit and shoes covered in the dry red earth. You know something, I couldn't think of a better way to say goodbye to someone. I'm sure Mum's resting in peace now. That was a kind thing you did for us, Johnny. I always knew you was a good lad. Harry, you don't know the half; the things I could tell you, but let's not go there, I smiled. Walking back between the headstones he told me about his new venture, renting out boats at the river gardens. I've finished with drugs. I don't deal anymore. She thought I was the perfect son, he said, stopping and looking back at her grave. Now it's too late, she's gone, and I keep telling myself it doesn't matter anymore, but it does.

Fuck it, he said to himself; follow me, Johnny, there's something I want to show you. We walked over to the far corner of the cemetery and stopped before a huge shiny black marble shrine, all gothic angels and scrolled letters. Do you know who this is? he asked me. I don't go around reading the headstones, Harry. Well, read this one, Johnny, you might find it interesting. Ricardo Valentine that was the name on the fancy headstone; Rizzo was buried here. What the hell was Harry playing at, did he know something? I killed him, Johnny, I heard Harry say. I turned to look at him in disbelief. It's true, he said, I shot him. I'm sorry, Johnny, but I had to tell someone. You shot him, Harry; are you sure? I asked him, wondering if this was some kind of sick joke. Jesus, course I'm sure I pulled the fucking trigger, and I just can't get it out of my mind; it's eating away at me. Harry, you didn't shoot Rizzo. Don't fuck about, Johnny, this is serious. I am serious, I shot him, but he didn't seem to hear me. Harry, I believe you when you say you shot someone, but it wasn't Rizzo. He said nothing, and in the silence a picture of what happened that night began to form in my mind. Just tell me what happened, Harry, and then I'll tell you all I know.

After the Derwent burnt down, Harry swore he was going to get his revenge. And a few days later with no idea of what he was going to do, he set off to find Rizzo. The very same night I paid him a visit. When he got there he suddenly realised how stupid he was, these people carried guns, what the hell was he going to do? It was then that fate took a hand, he saw someone coming down the fire escape. A black guy, it had to be Rizzo. He watched him take something out of the back of a Jag parked at the bottom of the steps. When the man went back up the steps, he followed him. Inside there was no sign of him, the place looked deserted until he came to an open door at the end of the passageway. Fucking hell, Johnny, it was like a scene from a horror film, there was blood everywhere. Then I saw some poor fucker slumped in a chair; half his head blown away. Suddenly I heard footsteps coming down the corridor. It was too late to get out, I hid behind the desk next to this dead guy, then I saw he had a gun in his hand. I don't know why, but I took the gun. Then I saw the black guy who I had followed come into the room. At first, he didn't see me, he was looking around the room, he seemed to be checking, making sure of something. And then he stopped, he must have noticed the gun was missing. You looking for this? I said, stepping out of the shadows, pointing the gun at him. Jesus fucking Christ, he said, who the fuck are you? I looked him in the eyes, Johnny, I swear I did. Rizzo? I asked him. Yeah, it's Rizzo, he said; honestly he said Rizzo. I pulled the trigger Johnny, I shot him.

That wasn't Rizzo, Harry. Rizzo was the dead guy in the chair. I shot him, it was an accident, I added quickly. So who did I shoot? Oh fuck, whoever it was, he was an innocent man. What have I done? He wasn't an innocent man, Harry, his name was Lenny, he worked for Rizzo. If someone didn't pay up on time he went around and broke a few bones, he beat up women, he killed people. If you hadn't killed him, Harry, he would have killed you.

Fuck, Harry, we got away with it, didn't we? Yeah, that's one thing I got right. I wiped the gun clean and put it back in Rizzo's hand. Made it look like Rizzo shot Lenny and then killed himself. The cops bought it, another drug deal gone wrong. Harry, you're a fucking genius, I said, putting my arm around his shoulder. He looked at me as though he was searching for some kind of redemption, but I didn't have any. They killed Carol, and they stole my record, I said instead.

The weeks went slowly by, and I still couldn't bring myself to tell Moira it was all over between us. That wasn't technically the truth; telling her wasn't the problem, I just couldn't be bothered. Somehow I had become trapped in limbo, waiting for Jill to come back. Every passing day without her made me realise how much I loved her. One day she would be back in my life.

The last week in October and the fair was in town, bringing with it a sense of excitement that never failed. The smells, the sounds, the sights, the gyppos, the weirdos, the thrill seekers, the fighters, all brought together under the dazzling whirling lights. I had never missed one night since I could remember, clutching pennies in one hand and holding on to my sister with the other. Smoking my first cigarette on my first proper date, with a blonde girl from another town. I was in awe of her beauty and her brains, so much more sophisticated than me that she seemed to come from some faraway exotic land and not the next little town five miles down the road. The happiest times had been only a year ago, walking around with Jill on my arm, feeling the warmth of her closeness running through my veins. Spending a fortune trying to win a flick knife, kissing her at the top of the big wheel, our faces almost in the stars. Was this really happening? I kept asking myself; it was real so very real, but somehow it had all fallen apart.

It was Saturday night, and the first frost was in the air. Moira had her arm through mine as we slowly wandered through the crowds. We stood and watched this year's new ride for a while, and once more I found myself thinking of this time last year. And then I saw her through the crowd only a few yards away; I had to stop myself from calling out to her. Until I realised it was probably my mind playing cruel tricks: she was just a vision. I closed my eyes, and when I opened them she was looking straight at me: she was real. We were set on a course that would take us inside our very souls.

Hiya, she said, stopping in front of us. Jill, I heard myself say, aware of Moira's grip on my arm tightening. She looked beautiful, she was beautiful and we looked straight into each other's eyes. Hello, I said, kneeling down in front of the pushchair, before we disappeared into each other's eyes. The little boy gave me a crooked grin when I pulled a face at him. What's his name? I asked her, getting to my feet. Nicky, she said, his name's Nicky. She looked at me again, this time as though she was looking for approval. Nicky, I said to myself, that's a good name; it suits him. Moira was gently pulling me away. Come on, Jonty, or we'll be late, she said. Yes, I must go as well, Jill said, smiling at Moira. We went our separate ways. I just wanted to go with her, with her and our son, but Moira was right here right now, and I had to deal with it. Moira was quiet the rest of the night; she knew it was all over, she always knew. He was a nice looking little boy, don't you think so? she asked. I nodded in agreement, my mind elsewhere. She was on her own then, and she wasn't wearing a wedding ring, I heard her say. Until then I had forgotten about her husband. Fucking hell, no wedding ring – she had chucked him. That makes everything easy for you, Moira said, stopping and turning to face me. What, don't be stupid, I heard myself say.

The rest of the night was awful; we hardly spoke to each other, until we were outside her house. You still love her, don't you? she suddenly said. It's written all over your face. That's daft, I said, trying to laugh it off. I know she loves you, I can tell. You seem to know everything, I said sarcastically, but you're wrong. All right, then, tell me that you don't love her, swear to me that you don't. Tears were slowly running down her face. I don't love her, I swear it. I love you, I said, taking her in my arms. She buried her face in my chest and sobbed. Why the fuck hadn't I told her? It couldn't have been any worse than this. I should have told her.

On Tuesday night I found myse!f once more standing across the road from Jill's house. It seemed almost a lifetime away since I had stood in exactly the same spot, before I had gone in and practically begged her to love me. Moira was at a evening class learning shorthand. I pictured her in my mind concentrating on those funny little dots and dashes. I should have felt at least a little guilt, but I felt none.

Jill opened the door before I had even knocked. See you later, she called back to someone. Closing the door behind her she leaned close and kissed me. The very closeness of her enveloped me in all the familiar things that now tumbled from my memory. I loved her so much; I could hardly breath for fear of losing this moment. Where have you been? I've been waiting for you every night. I didn't think you were going to come at all. She put her hands up inside my jacket and pushed me back against the side of the house. This was the very same place we had stood on that hot summer night. She must have been thinking the same thoughts as me. Do you remember? she smiled. I kissed her forehead and the tip of her nose, and kissed away the tears that had begun to fall. I'm so sorry, Jonty, she sobbed.

We walked around all the streets and alleyways we knew so well, until we found ourselves once more in our bus shelter. I'm sorry, she said again. Stop saying you're sorry, you've got nothing to be sorry for. I'm sorry for running away. I couldn't stand the thought of making you unhappy again, she said. It's all right, Jill ,you're not the only one who ran away. She looked at me, her eyes still full of tears. That night you rang me, you mean. I knew something was wrong. It doesn't matter anymore; that's all in the past. I won't ever let you go again, she said, holding me tight. The baby's yours, Jonty, you know that, don't you? Nicky's our son. Please tell me you believe me. You saw him; he looks just like you. It's all right, Jill, I've always known, but now I really know. I started to cry. Crying was becoming a habit. What will you tell Moira? she asked me as we stood by her front gate. The truth, I'll tell her the truth. Do you want me to come with you? she said. I feel terrible; poor Moira. Don't worry about it, I said; I think she half knows anyway. You know something, if we hadn't got back together I think I would have become a nun, taken a vow of silence and served my penance.

They were just coming out of the college gates. I could see Moira talking to another girl in the lighted corridor. She looked up and smiled when I walked through the door; this was going to be harder than I thought. Sorry I'm late, I said, kissing her. That's all right, she started to say, and then she stopped mid-sentence. She was staring at me, her whole expression changing to a look of horror before my eyes. What is it, what's wrong? I said, reaching out for her hand. Don't you come near me, she shouted, backing away. People passing by were staring at us, and I could feel myself turning red. You've been with her. My God, you've been with her; how could you? She started to scream as though she had just realised what she had said. We need to talk, Moira, please let's go somewhere and talk it through, I reasoned. She looked me in the eye and there were no tears. You told me you loved me, and I believed you, she said. I didn't know what to say. I tried, Moira, I really tried. You know something, Jonty, I would have done anything for you, I would have given my life for you, but it doesn't matter. She shrugged her shoulders and turned around and walked out of my life. For a few moments the silence continued, all eyes on me to see what I would do. Suddenly, just as though someone turned on a switch, the world came to life again, the sound of voices and the movement of people filled the room. The girl, who she had been talking to, was still standing in the same spot. I'm sorry about that, I said, turning to look at her, I really don't know what that was all about. She reached over and touched my neck; I guess Moira didn't give you that, she said before walking away. I stood for a moment with my hand on the place on my neck where she had touched me. Inside the toilets I looked in the mirror. The love bite was big and dark red; I must have known it was there, so did Jill. Looking again in the mirror I saw the bus shelter just a couple of hours ago; were we really so callous and cruel to have done this to her? You cunt, I said to it.

One month later me and Jill and Nicky moved into a one-bed flat above a jeweller's shop in the high street; it wasn't much but it was a place of our own. It was the same jewellery shop that Moira and me had stood looking in the window of many a night, picking out a ring for our engagement. It was hard for a while; we were young and scared, and love was such a powerful thing to deal with. Trying to deal with falling in love at so young an age had taken us both on a long tortuous diversion.

Chapter Nineteen

JILL

The days and weeks turned into months; it was a time like no other before or since, a time I would not change for the world. Ours always had been a raw ragged on-the-edge kind of love, an exciting love, and so it remained. He was the love of my life, my every breath, my very reason for being on this planet. To think that I had hurt him so much made me cry silent tears as he slept, until I came to realise we had to come through all of this to reach the love we had. It must have been written somewhere: this love would happen no matter what; we would always find each other. Summer came around again and life felt good. Moira was back with Tony. Jonty said they were made for each other. We had seen them a couple of times; the first time, Moira had looked the other way, and who could blame her? The second time she smiled and said hello, easing the burden of guilt we both felt. Jonty was playing football again semiprofessional, and the extra money he made had given us enough for the deposit on a house – just a two up, two down terrace. We were so excited, lying awake most of the night, talking through all our plans and silly little ideas. Andy Bailey came home, and him and Jonty talked about reforming The Pulsators. It was a part of his life I knew nothing about, something that made me sad, just like that phone call on that cold winter's night when I knew he was in trouble, and I ran away. It would be years before that missing period would be pieced together, something I would be glad to know. Harry rebuilt the Derwent Club on the site of the old one, and soon built up a good reputation with the new crowd. He and Jonty seemed very close, and he was always asking us to come along to the new club. We never did go; Jonty always made some excuse. The place is clean, Johnny, no more dealers, no more playing gangsters, I overheard Harry saying one day. After what happened the last time you know I would never do that again, Harry said. It's not that, Harry, I know you wouldn't go down that route again; it's just not my scene anymore, Jonty told him. Well, if you ever change your mind we've got a great DJ; Roothy plays all the stuff you and him used to like. Roothy's back at the Derwent? That's great, Harry. How is he? Just you look after him. Don't worry, Johnny, I will, Harry smiled. Why don't you go? I said to him after Harry had gone. I don't mind. He smiled at me: I know you don't, but honestly I don't want to go; maybe it's me still living in the past, but I prefer the old Derwent.

Everything seemed to be fitting into place, and we were just a week away from moving into our house when I found out I was pregnant again. This time it was planned, and both of us could not have been any happier; this time we were together to share every moment. Wednesday night, I went along to see The Pulsators rehearsing in the upstairs function room of the Queen's Head; it was the first time I had heard them, Jonty had kept me away, saying they weren't good enough yet. It was a magical night. I thought they were brilliant, completely taking me by surprise. Andy could certainly play the guitar, and the two new boys on drums and bass were really good. Barry, a lad we had known at school, had become their unofficial manager, full of infectious energy and enthusiasm. Barry had brought along his reel-to-reel tape recorder, and that night he recorded three songs; the three best tracks they played he explained to me: Del Shannon's *Kelly*, The Small Faces' *Sorry She's Mine*, and of course The Carnaby and *Jump and Dance,* my favourite record. The copy Jonty had given to me was almost worn away I had played it so much; that record just seemed to say everything about that special time in our lives. That night, as we walked home talking excitedly about the group, he said something strange, just threw it into the conversation. I almost didn't hear it, this little downer in amongst all the happy chatter. I must have heard it because now I can't get it out of my mind. You know, Jill, every time things are going so well, I always think something bad is going to come along and spoil everything.

Sunday afternoon we spent in the river gardens, lying on the grass listening to the brass band and watching Nicky happily running after the ducks. Looking back in my mind,

I see that day so clearly, remembering every second, each tiny detail almost down to the blades of grass on which we lay. But sometimes I think I am imagining it all, until it quickly fades away. On the way home, that something bad happened, that something we laughed away. If only we had gone home the normal way, but we wanted to get an ice cream for Nicky. They had been drinking that lunchtime, my husband and two of his friends, the smell of beer on their hate-filled tongues. The car pulled up to the kerb slightly in front of us, and even before I saw who was in it I knew something was wrong. They got out and stood across the pavement, blocking our way. Well, this is all very cosy, he said; playing happy families, are we? Leave us alone, Pete; just go home please, I reasoned with him. Well hello, dear, and how are you? he said, turning to me. A little birdie tells me you're up the fucking duff again. Jonty made a move towards him; I put my hand on his arm and pulled him back. That's my wife you've been fucking, he said to Jonty; mind you, you're welcome to her, fucking whore. Nicky started crying at all the raised voices. Come here, son, Pete said, holding out his arms to Nicky. Don't you come anywhere near him, I shouted, he's not your son; he never was and he never will be. There was silence for a moment as he stood trying to work out what to do next, the eyes of his two mates on him. Come on, Jonty, let's go, I said, taking his hand. You ain't going nowhere, Pete sneered, not until I fucking say so. Hey, just leave it, I heard Jonty say calmly; we don't want any trouble, now do we? Pete turned to his mates and started to laugh. Did you hear that, lads? The hard man don't want any trouble. I felt his hand slip from mine, and before I could stop him he hit Pete in the gut, and when he doubled over he hit him again on the side of his face.

JONTY

It was a mistake, a fucking big mistake; they were supposed to run away but instead his two mates came wading in, fists flying. I was on my hands and knees when I saw it coming out of the corner of my eye: someone kicked me full force on the side of my head. They say your life passes before you when you die. Does your death pass before you when you are born? It seems I lived my life in denial, and now I was paying for it, for I knew all along the final outcome. All those dreams I could never remember, and now I was stuck in one, trapped in an eternal nightmare.

They all came to see me. I can hear them talking to me, talking about me. So close I can feel them: Mum, Dad, my sister, Roothy, Harry, Nicky, and Jill, always in black and white, a nun, until I realise everything in my world is black and white; there are no Technicolor landscapes, just black and white ghosts. Jill is not a nun; she has not taken a vow of silence, even though she prays a lot. She talks to me; always she says she's sorry; I tell her there is nothing to be sorry for, but of course she cannot hear me. She places a baby across my chest, our baby, a baby girl. I feel one tiny tear plop on to my face, and the white begins to fade. The last flicker of my almost dead brain remembers our claim to fame. The night Jill and me were thrown out of the pub for playing *Sir Geoffrey*

Saved The World fifteen times, one after the other. I was just trying to make them see, it was so beautiful. Well, we got it. The good ghosts are here, and as my world turns black I know I'm smiling.

JILL

He lay in a coma for six months. Kelly came early, she had to see her daddy. Jonty's mum turned up at the hospital the day before Kelly was born, and she held in her hand what appeared to be a bundle of paper tied with string. I found this, Jill, she said, holding out the bundle for me. I think you should read it. I held it in my hand and looked down at the title written in big bold capitals, *Jump and Dance.* I turned the pages, all of them written in Jonty's familiar handwriting. That night I read Jonty's story, our story of a short life together, trying to make sense of being so much in love, all the hurt and pain, all the laughter, all the good times. Even when we were apart, it seems we spent that time aching to be together. At four o'clock that morning I went into labour, and once our little daughter was born I knew what we had to do. The end had been written long before it arrived; now it was here it did not seem so bad. Jonty hated funerals, so the less said the better. He wouldn't want any fuss; neither did I, but I couldn't stop them. All those people who packed the church; all the Mods were close to tears as they filed outside with The Who crackling through a speaker *The Kids are Alright.*

It's now almost a year since that day. I moved into the house we had bought. It's a struggle to pay the bills but I have a job in the evenings back at the factory where Jonty used to wait for me when the five o'clock whistle went. Nicky and Kelly are my whole life now, although some people don't understand that. I always tell them it's too soon, and they smile at me knowingly. Maybe it's just me, but I know I will never find the kind of love I have known ever again; anything else would just be second best, and I ask myself, would it be fair? But who knows. I have the tape that Barry made of The Pulsators, just those three songs, but I still haven't played it, and I don't think I ever will. There aren't so many Mods about these days, and I don't know what Jonty would make of the music. All I know for certain is, I was lucky I'd had love.

POSTSCRIPT

ROOTHY

Died from liver failure, due to alcoholism, 1991, aged forty-one, left behind two ex-wives and three children.

HARRY

Died from a heart attack, May 1968, aged forty-nine.

OMO

Lost contact.

JONTY'S MUM & DAD

Dad died of one too many heart attacks, June 1996 aged seventy-four. Mum died nine months later, complications from a heart valve operation, March 1997, aged seventy.

MOIRA

Married the nice young man she deserved, still married, now sixty-four years old.

ANDY

Moved back to London to pursue a career in music, changed The Pulsators name to The Unknown. Turned his attention to writing about music and became a writer for a well-known music paper. Married Ingrid, still married.

SUE

Married the Pretend Mod, divorced four years later. No children, remained friends with Jill.

VIV

Married Kenny. They divorced.

TEDDY

Married Mary. Still married.

NICKY

Now forty-nine years old, married with two children, rides a Vespa 150cc with all the chrome and mirrors. Taught himself the guitar, and formed The New Pulsators, sometimes they play *I'm In Love With Carol White.*

KELLY

Housewife and children's book writer. Looks just like her mum.

JILL

Never remarried, two long-term relationships. Died from cancer aged sixty-four.